Stories from Life's Other Side

People Living on the Margins of Modern Day Society

Kay Matthews

SUNSTONE PRESS

SANTA FE

Sunstone books may be purchased for educational, business, or sales promotional use.
For information please write: Special Markets Department, Sunstone Press,
P.O. Box 2321, Santa Fe, New Mexico 87504-2321.
Cover photograph by _______________________
Book and cover design › Vicki Ahl
Body typeface › Garamond Pro
Printed on acid-free paper
∞
eBook 978-1-61139-459-7

Library of Congress Cataloging-in-Publication Data

Names: Matthews, Kay, author.
Title: Stories from life's other side : people living on the margins of
   modern day society / by Kay Matthews.
Description: Santa Fe : Sunstone Press, [2016]
Identifiers: LCCN 2016001768 (print) | LCCN 2016011154 (ebook) | ISBN
   9781632931184 (softcover : acid-free paper) | ISBN 9781611394597 ()
Classification: LCC PS3613.A84865 A6 2016 (print) | LCC PS3613.A84865 (ebook)
   | DDC 813/.6--dc23
LC record available at http://lccn.loc.gov/2016001768

SUNSTONE PRESS IS COMMITTED TO MINIMIZING OUR ENVIRONMENTAL IMPACT ON THE PLANET.
THE PAPER USED IN THIS BOOK IS FROM RESPONSIBLY MANAGED FORESTS. OUR PRINTER HAS RECEIVED CHAIN OF CUSTODY
(COC) CERTIFICATION FROM: THE FOREST STEWARDSHIP COUNCIL™ (FSC®), PROGRAMME FOR THE ENDORSEMENT OF FOREST
CERTIFICATION™ (PEFC™), AND THE SUSTAINABLE FORESTRY INITIATIVE® (SFI®).
THE FSC® COUNCIL IS A NON-PROFIT ORGANIZATION, PROMOTING THE ENVIRONMENTALLY APPROPRIATE, SOCIALLY BENEFICIAL
AND ECONOMICALLY VIABLE MANAGEMENT OF THE WORLD'S FORESTS. FSC® CERTIFICATION IS RECOGNIZED INTERNATIONALLY
AS A RIGOROUS ENVIRONMENTAL AND SOCIAL STANDARD FOR RESPONSIBLE FOREST MANAGEMENT.

WWW.SUNSTONEPRESS.COM
SUNSTONE PRESS / POST OFFICE BOX 2321 / SANTA FE, NM 87504-2321 /USA
(505) 988-4418 / ORDERS ONLY (800) 243-5644 / FAX (505) 988-1025

Stories from
Life's Other Side

Contents

Preface

These stories are dedicated to the people I've lived with, worked with, or crossed paths with on the many roads we've traveled. The time and place of the stories largely determine content. The place is mostly New Mexico, where I've lived all my adult life. The time began in the tumultuous years of the 1970s when all kinds of people were living all kinds of lives: on the economic margins of middle class society; in the midst of cultural transformations that changed the world as we knew it; in the day to day grind of making do. There's some mourning of what we've lost, some soul searching about what we want, but a lot of acceptance of what we have.

The boundaries between truth telling and interpreting are as blurred here as they are in our every day lives. The standard disclaimer, that any resemblance of characters in this work of fiction to actual people is strictly coincidental, can be slightly modified: the characters in this work of fiction are born in familiarity but given flight by imagination.

The Pet Chicken

My friend Ursula keeps a pet chicken in her house. I go over there one day to borrow some milk and I see this chicken walking around under the kitchen table. I ask her son, Joey, who is sitting at the table, why the chicken is in the house.

"Because it has a pink head," he says.

This chicken does indeed have a pink head, but that's still no reason to let a chicken be in the house, I t hink. Later, when I see that Ursula is home, I go back over to find out about the chicken.

"The kids' babysitter gave them two baby chicks for Easter," Ursula says.

"You mean there's another chicken in the house, too?" I ask.

"No, Anton drowned his baby chick in the humidifier, so just Ellen's is left. It wasn't so bad when it was just a chick, its droppings were little and I could sweep them out the door. But now..."

"Why don't you give it to someone who keeps chickens in a pen?" I ask.

"Every time I tell Ellen that we need to find a home for her chicken she starts to cry and carry on about taking her pet away from her. When she comes home from school she holds it in her lap and it makes these little clicking noises down in its throat, like a cat purring. And it sleeps under her bed."

"Maybe you could build a little cage out in the yard and keep it there as an outside pet."

The chicken follows Ursula to the refrigerator and a series of cackles rises higher and higher in pitch until the door closes again.

"What are you feeding this chicken—hamburger?" I ask. "And by the way, why is its head pink?"

"They put dye in the eggs before the chicks are born so they can sell them at Easter. I guess the dye only got on this one's head."

"That's disgusting."

"I know, but Flora, the kids' babysitter, goes in for that kind of stuff," Ursula says. "And you know how hard it is to find good babysitters."

Ursula knows all about babysitters, having juggled her kids around from one to another over the years as her life fell apart in stages. First, Joey's father left them when Joey was three to move in with a palm reader in Alamita who fancied herself a curandera, a "healer" in the Mexican tradition, although she was also rumored to be a witch. Ursula was sure she was, because Frank, her husband, came home one day and out of the blue, so to speak, announced he was leaving Ursula for Naomi.

It wasn't as if he was bettering his circumstances by doing so. Ursula, Joey, and Frank lived in a crumbling adobe in Rositas, but at least it had electricity, running water, and the semblance of respectability. Naomi's crumbling adobe in Alamita lacked all amenities, unless you could say a spectacular view was worth no water, electricity, or phone. Ursula and I drove by her place once, after Frank had left, to see where he was living.

"You can't just pretend someone is dead because they're not sitting across the table from you anymore," Ursula said.

Naomi's house stood in the middle of a pasture, noticeably free of wires and the 20th century in its picturesque setting of mountains as backdrop, cottonwoods for shade, and grazing goats for character.

"I guess curanderas don't make any more money now than they ever did," Ursula said.

"I'm sorry this happened," I said. "Probably won't last."

"Doesn't matter if it doesn't," Ursula said. "Joey and I are through with men who leave women."

So Ursula goes into the ceramic button business full time. Trained as an artist, like so many before her, she finds crafts her reality. She does make beautiful buttons in the shape of ladybugs, tarantulas, stars, and crescent moons, and maybe it satisfies some of her artistic desires, but she harbors dreams of galleries instead of booths at craft fairs. Of course, one meets a lot of people at craft shows, people who often live like you do, on the edge, close to the wire, hand to mouth, as they say. And it isn't long before Ursula hooks up with such a man who displays painted eggs in his booth. His name is Rico and he soon moves into Ursula's crumbling adobe in Rositas, and the three of them, Joey, Ursula, and Rico travel around to fairs with their buttons and eggs and Frank disappears from her heart as well as her table.

Then, after a few years, Rico makes it known that he'd like to be a real father, not just Joey's stepfather, and Ursula soon has not only one new baby but two new babies in two years. Unfortunately, the second baby is born with a mind not of this world, and Ursula has to quit making buttons and traveling around to craft shows with Rico to devote her time to Ellen and Anton.

I go over sometimes to help entertain Anton, who wants attention from someone all the time because he is unable to manufacture interest from within. Ursula is his main interest, and sometimes she doesn't want to be.

"Ellen is so jealous of Anton I think if I ever left them alone she would stuff him in a drawer and nail it shut," Ursula says.

"Why doesn't Rico take her with him when he goes to shows so she can have some extra attention away from Anton?" I ask.

"Rico is unable to pay attention to small children longer than a five minute pony ride on his knee. I wonder how you can know these things about husbands who leave wives for curanderas or husbands who make lousy fathers. Rico tells me he's not happy with this situation. I ask him, who is, but you tell me what we're going to do about it."

But Rico has nothing more to say. In fact, he loses his ability to speak altogether, and commits himself to a psychiatric hospital for observation and diagnosis. The observation takes over a year, and the diagnosis confirms he needs more observation. So Ursula gets another divorce and once again settles for the single life.

"At least this time I'm losing one to a whole institution of quackery, not just an individual participant," Ursula says.

Out of necessity Ursula becomes aware of social programs designed to prevent single mothers with three children from starving. And because of Anton, she qualifies for state paid babysitters and special school programs designed to anchor Anton in the here and now.

"This time I'm not going to make buttons," Ursula says, when she finds she has five days a week without children from nine to three. "I'm going to paint. That way, you stay home in your studio and don't meet men."

She doesn't have a studio so she paints in her bedroom, one more reason for keeping the space clear. To buy paints she borrows money from Joey, who works in a fast food joint after school. For awhile she manages to paint a picture or two that please her, but when you have no money and no one to do all the things that need to be done because you have no money, things start to fall apart. Cars break down and there's no one to put them up on the backyard jacks and fix them. A window gets broken and cardboard put in its place. And a pink chicken takes over the house.

I go over to Ursula's house a week after I first see the chicken, and it's still there. It now has brown feathers coming out over its body along with its still pink head. I do notice a small wire cage sitting in the front yard with nothing in it.

"So how's the chicken doing?" I ask.

"Don't talk to me about that chicken," Ursula says, standing over some stew on the stove. "Ralph brought over that cage and put it out in the yard, but when I tried to put the chicken in there it ran around in circles and cackled at the top of its lungs until I couldn't stand it anymore."

Ralph is Ursula's new boyfriend.

"I thought you'd sworn off men," I said, when she first told me about him.

"I swore off marrying men," she said. "I only let this one stay over on Thursday and Sunday nights. That way we're only having an affair, not a relationship. It's kind of fun having an affair. I've never really had one before."

Having an affair is useful, too, as Ralph proves to be an excellent auto mechanic, plumber, and carpenter. Apparently he also knows how to relate to children, because the next time I come over, the pink-headed chicken is outside in a cute little fenced in yard with a rooster, a large red hen, and five other baby chickens, all of normal color.

"I see you managed to get Ellen's chicken outside," I say.

"I didn't, Ralph did," Ursula says. "I really didn't want any more chickens, but when he explained his plan to me I couldn't say no."

"His plan?"

"Yeah, he says that you have to present kids with options, just like you do with adults. So he tells Ellen that instead of the pink-headed chicken living in our family it needs a family of its own, a mother and father and five siblings. And then it won't be expected to conform to our way of life when in its own family. It can shit all over the pen and peck at anything it wants to."

"Sounds like this guy has a way with kids."

"He should," Ursula says. "He's got two of his own."

"Uh oh," I say. "And a wife?"

"An ex-wife, so it's okay. Neither of us is ready for five, so Thursdays and Sundays are fine."

There's a show down the road in Alamita for local artists, and Ursula hangs her paintings there for all to stare at, critique, and—hopefully—buy. She paints very colorful pictures of exotic animals and plants that grow in her imagination, like Lewis Carroll's Cheshire cat. She's yet to paint a chicken with a pink head.

"How's it going?" I ask, meaning, have you sold anything yet.

"Sue Barker just asked me if she could buy one of my $300 paintings on time," Ursula says.

"Which one?" I ask.

"That one," she says, pointing to one of my favorites, a black flower growing out of a zebra-like creature.

"Sue Barker can afford to give you the whole $300 at once, you know," I say.

"I know. It's always so damn hard for people—even rich people—to spend money on something you can't wear, plug in, or sniff up your nose. So she's giving me fifty dollars a month for six months."

"That's tacky," I say.

"Beggars can't be choosers," she says, "or it's back to buttons."

"How's Ralph?"

"He's okay. Except he went out and got some geese to put in with the chickens and every time I go in to feed them they try to attack me. Ellen won't go anywhere near them."

"I guess that finally solves the problem of the pet chicken."

"No such luck. Now she's bugging me to bring the chicken back in the house because she says the geese are going to peck it to death."

"Have the geese been pecking the chickens?"

"No, they only like human flesh," Ursula says.

"Why don't you tell Ralph to get rid of the geese?"

"I did. He says he got them for my protection. He worries about me except on Sundays and Thursdays."

"Sounds like he's getting kind of possessive," I say. "Besides which, since when are geese watchdogs?"

"You're right—and he's right. Every time someone comes over those geese start honking like hell and won't shut-up until Anton throws rocks at them."

"Life's getting complicated again, isn't it?" I say.

"And all I want is to have enough to eat, spend some time with my kids, and sell a few paintings." Ursula says.

Sue Barker's fifty dollars a month enables Ursula to buy paint with impunity, and a new, spiffy portfolio in which to take her work around to the galleries. But it's the museum, not the galleries, that decides to give her the break she's been looking for all these many years. Realism, especially Ursula's kind of hyperbolic realism, is back in vogue, and the museum pays her several thousand dollars for a painting depicting the germination of a magic seed.

Ursula has me over for coffee and cake one afternoon to celebrate her windfall.

"That's what I think of it as—a windfall," she says. "Not the culmination of years of hard work, paying my dues. Maybe it's the only $2,000 I'll ever see at one time."

"Being bought by a museum to be hung in their permanent collection ain't shabby," I say.

"Then why do I feel like my life's still just as marginal, just as close to the edge as ever?" she asks. "The money was spent before I ever got it—a new carburetor for an old car, double glazing on the north window, a new toilet. Somehow I always think that the money I earn for my art should never be spent on such mundane things. It should be for the extras, the stuff that makes life worth living. But here I am, still worrying about next month's bills, whether the food stamps will make it until the end of the month, whether Ralph will show up Sunday as usual."

"I thought you two were grooving right along."

"I guess we are," Ursula says. "Too much so, it seems. But that doesn't stop me worrying. My track record is not that great, you know."

"Why don't you relax and enjoy it," I say.

"I don't know," she says. "Guess I'm just sitting around waiting for the next crisis."

It arrives in the form of Rico. He appears one day and tells Ursula that the only thing that can save him from annihilation is their remarriage and her lifelong devotion. She asks him if he's been released from the hospital, and he tells her they let him out during the day so he can make eggs. They figure it's good occupational therapy. If Ursula will only let him move back in with her they'll let him out for good.

"But you committed yourself, Rico," Ursula says. "You can leave whenever you want."

"I can't make that decision," Rico says. "I need you to make it for me."

"I can't do that, " Ursula says.

"Then I'm going to move in next door until you let me back in the house," he says.

"I thought you said you couldn't make the decision to leave the hospital unless I made it for you," Ursula says.

"Next door is close enough for now," he says. "I'm sure you'll make the right decision."

I go over to Ursula's house to see why the U-Haul truck is parked outside. Joey is carrying big, bare, canvasses out of the house and stacking them in the trailer.

"Where's Ursula?" I ask.

"She's out in the chicken pen killing a chicken."

"The pink-headed one?"

"I don't know. I hope so."

I find her in the pen with a chicken's neck pinned down under a broom. She reaches down and chops off its head just as I open the gate. I can't really tell if it's the pink one.

"What's going on?" I ask.

"I'm killing the chicken," Ursula says. "Then I'm moving all my stuff to Alamita and getting out of this black hole."

"But what about your house?"

"I'm renting it to Ralph and his two kids. He wanted to move in anyway, so now he can—without me and Joey and Ellen and Anton and with Rico next door."

"What are you going to do in town?"

"I'm going to paint. I'm going to have a clean house with no chicken in it. I'm going to have nothing to do with my neighbors. And I'm going to have no more illusions."

"Good luck," I say.

"I think I've finally figured out it takes more than luck," Ursula says, throwing the chicken over the fence into a pile of weeds. Grasshoppers descend upon it voraciously, and by the time the U-Haul is loaded there is no trace of a pink-headed chicken in Ursula's house.

Janis

There's a famous photograph, from around 1968, of Janis Joplin in her boas sprawled next to the adobe wall of a house in Truchas, New Mexico. Maybe if she hadn't died an untimely death at the age of twenty-eight, she would have bought one of the old crumbling adobes in Truchas, like other hippies were doing then, and on periodic visits back to this mountain town she and I would hop in her '57 Chevy convertible and go cruising down to Española, the lowrider capital of New Mexico. Imagine what it would be like to cruise the main drag of Española on a Friday night with Janis Joplin, in line with the brothers whose blood runs thick with mag wheels, hydraulic lifts, and iridescent paint jobs. I'm sure Janis would have been granted honorary lowrider membership.

It's the 1990s now, and I just read in the paper about Kurt Cobain's mother saying, "Oh no, he went and did a dumb thing like those others," after they'd found him dead with a self-inflicted gunshot wound. Rock 'n' roll had Brian Jones, Jim Morrison, Jimi, and Janis, now punk and grunge have their own fatalities. I'm not even sure I'd know a song by Nirvana, Kurt Cobain's group, if I heard it, but I always sympathize with tortured souls. To this day, I'm sure I could have saved Janis if I'd just had the chance.

I live in a village just down the road from Truchas, with my wife and kids, whom I love dearly, but that doesn't keep me from thinking about Janis from time to time. As a matter of fact, my wife kind of looks like her, especially in old sixties pictures with her hair in her face, grinning out at the camera. She's a big fan of Janis, too, and we often put Cheap Thrills on the stereo and dance around the living room, much to our kids' amusement. Sometimes I even fantasize about being Janis's record producer as well. Every time I hear a certain song I think she could have sung the shit out of, like "I Don't Have to Crawl," which Roseanne Cash sings beautifully but Janis could have broken your heart with, I realize I missed my calling. Or imagine Janis and Marvin Gaye singing "Sexual Healing." The possibilities are endless.

My Española fantasy goes something like this. After spending the morning in my sound studio (built down in the lower pasture where the hay grows three feet tall) mixing Janis's latest album, I'd drive on over to Truchas for some Friday afternoon recreation. Janis would be hanging out at her artfully restored adobe house with any number of people, but she'd be very happy to see me.

"Hey, man, how're you doing?" she'd call out from her reclined position on the couch, shot of Southern Comfort in hand. "How's my record coming, man?" (I have a hard time imaging her saying, "How's my CD coming, man?")

"It's gonna be the best thing you've ever done, Janis, it's gonna bust everybody's balls, I'm telling you. But in the meantime, let's run on down to Española. I need some R & R, and I don't mean rock 'n' roll."

"I'm too much for you, man, much too much," Janis laughs. To everyone else she says, "This guy's got me doing stuff I never knew I could do and it's going to be great! Now someone go run and bring the Chevy around the front 'cause Janis is going to do some cruisin'!"

We climb in her cherried-out, red-and-white '57 Chevy convertible and head down the Truchas mountain road that kills drunk drivers every year on its tricky curves. But Janis handles the Chevy beautifully, her hand resting on the steering wheel, her arm on the window, her hair blowing in the breeze. The green mountain pastures give way to red-colored sandstone rocks carved to mounded Jell-O molds by eons of wind and rain and sun.

It's hot down on the Española asphalt, where not a shrub or tree dares to decorate the extended strip mall that is, despite other cities' claim to the name, the city of no illusions: Big Rock Shopping Center on the left, Big-O Tires on the right, Salazar Funeral Home on the Left, Lujan Funeral Home on the Right. We check into the cruising line in the middle of town, where you turn right to Taco Bell or left to Jumbo Burger, where real tacos are made.

But Janis isn't interested in eating. She puts on her plumed hat, sinks down in her seat, and slows to cruising speed. One of the main lowrider games is to slow the flow of traffic behind you by assuring that every green light is missed, every opportunity to pass is squelched, and any attempt to turn left is rendered impossible. A lot of the traffic behind you consists of Anglo tourists anxious to get from Taos to Santa Fe or Santa Fe to Taos and who can't believe they have to go through Española to do this. Where are the boutiques, where are the Indians sitting around selling their wares, where are the fern-filled restaurants serving pineapple chutney tacos covered with chipotle sauce?

Janis and I join in. Our conversation focuses on this juxtaposition of BMWs and lowriders.

"Where do these assholes get off driving around in their fancy cars with their air conditioning going full blast in Española, man," Janis says, pointing with her chin at the car next to us, which happens to be a Range Rover. She turns to face the woman in the passenger seat and yells, "Roll down your window, honey, and get a whiff of fumes like the rest of us. You think you're too good to breathe our air? You gotta bring your sterilized air with you, just like you bring your sterilized lives? Go back to Texas or California."

"May I remind you, Janis, that you are from both Texas and California," I say.

"Yeah, but I'm a free spirit, man, and when I'm in California I sing rock 'n' roll and roller skate at Venice Beach, but when I'm in New Mexico, man, I cruise the camino, entiendes?" She pulls ahead of the Range Rover and quickly cuts across into its lane, slowing down even more. "Maybe those Range Rover fucks will get a little local culture by osmosis, even if they are deaf, dumb, and blind."

At the next light, Janis stops next to a Chevy Impala lowrider aglow with orange flames. As soon as the driver sees her he extends his hand over to me for a soul-brother handshake. "Hey, Janis, what you doing down here? You supposed to be up there in Trrrruchas, making some of that good rock 'n' roll."

"Gimme a break, man, don't I get to fuck around a little like the rest of you fuck-heads down here, lowriding your lives away?" she yells back at him.

I expect him to pull out his gun and blow us away. Instead, he throws back his head and laughs uproariously. The light changes to green and he tears off, laying a patch.

"Just how do you get off talking to a vato like that?" I ask Janis as we slowly proceed up the street. "I thought we were dead."

"I can get away with anything, honey," Janis says, popping a wad of Juicy Fruit into her mouth. "Seriously, man, these guys don't care what I say to them because they know I'm one of them. They know I was looked down on and spit on and considered scum because I was different, man. So I cultivated it, I flaunted it, I shoved it in their faces. Why do you think these guys drive around in these outrageous cars looking like banditos with their red bandanas and baggy pants? Because it's in your *face*, man!"

Then suddenly, inexplicably, Janis Joplin bursts into tears.

"Janis, what's the matter, honey?" I ask. "Don't cry, please don't cry." Like all men, I can't stand to see a woman cry, but I can't bear seeing Janis Joplin cry.

"Oh, man, everything is such a goddamned mess," Janis says, the tears streaming down her cheeks. "Here I am, almost fifty years old still struttin' my stuff on stage like I was twenty-five, only I got varicose veins and bags under my eyes, and they ain't from smoking numbers and staying up all night."

"What are you talking about, you look great," I say. This fantasy I've concocted about cruising with Janis has her looking like she did at twenty-eight, of course, with a thin, supple body, long, fly-a-way hair, rings on her fingers and stars in her eyes. I don't know what she'd look like at fifty. That's not part of the equation.

"So many of them are gone, man," Janis says, continuing to weep. "Otis, Marvin, Jim, Pigpen, Tammy, Jimi, John. They died before they had to figure out how to do it for twenty more years. I mean, how do you know when it ain't your time anymore, man? How do you know when you ain't got anything more to say, and what you've been saying is just a bunch of shit? Only all those people are out there screaming in your face that you're wonderful and beautiful and talented and how do you give that up, man?"

"I guess it's kind of like the writer who has one good novel in him but he keeps putting out drivel because he doesn't know what else to do," I say. "But you've got something new, I know, because I've got it on tape."

"It's all the same, man," she wails. "We all think we have something to say so we can feel like we're important, that we count for something, that we matter. But all we are are masses of ectoplasm, waiting to be squashed."

Wait a minute. This is my fantasy and I don't at all like the way it's going. I don't want to be hearing this stuff from Janis Joplin. And I don't have to. So I put us back on the highway, headed towards Truchas, but this time through the Rio Grande gorge, where the river is running high and wide alongside the curvy canyon road that Janis travels with finesse.

"I love this place, man," she calls into the wind. "Ain't it great to be living here, making great music, with a great producer." She slaps my knee. "Let's drive up to your place and listen to what you've got so far."

"So you think what we've done so far is okay?" I ask her. I can't quite forget the preceding diatribe, even if it was just my imagination ("running away with me").

"It's better than okay, man, it's great, like I said. I mean, after twenty years in this business—jeez, it must be thirty years in this business, qué no?—you gotta take some chances and do some different stuff and grow a little, you know what I mean. Of course you know what I mean, man, you're helping me do it. Not that I'm knocking what I've been doing, which is rock 'n' roll from its soul-black roots, and that I've been doing it for as long as I can be the best that I can. But there's a whole lot of music out there just waiting for Janis to put her stamp on, and you and me are going to do it, man."

At Embudo we turn off the canyon highway and head back up into the mountains. The road travels through Dixon, an old Hispano village turned artsy-fartsy, with willow furniture, statice wreaths, and silver jewelry supporting the aging hippie entrepreneurs who've managed to hang onto the rural life without having to go back to school to become teachers or social workers like their parents. Past Dixon, the road climbs through Picuris Pueblo land and on into the mountain villages greened by acequias that have been delivering snow-fed spring water to farms for hundreds of years. Janis raises two fingers from the steering wheel to salute each passing car, a holdover from when everybody actually knew everybody else in the passing car. To not wave would be an unforgivable offense.

Janis turns off the main highway onto the dirt road that leads to my house. She again slows to cruising speed, this time to avoid shaking the front end loose on the ruts and potholes that keep out the BMWs and Jaguars. Of course the Range Rovers have solved the problem of how to travel the backcountry roads while still maintaining the style to which they are accustomed, but so far not too many of them have had reason to travel my road that leads to no boutiques, restaurants, or gift shops. No espresso bar delivers to my studio.

My wife delivers homemade tortillas, though. As soon as Janis and I are inside, cueing up the tape to listen to the latest recording, she appears with a towel-draped plate stacked with fresh, warm, whole-wheat tortillas. Janis gives her a big hug and slathers a hot one with raspberry jam.

"What a great old lady you got, man," Janis says, stuffing her mouth with tortilla. Then, all of a sudden, she's crying again.

"I ain't never had an old man who really loved me," she cries. "And I ain't ever going to have a man who really loves me. All they want is a piece of my ass."

"But you've known so many interesting men, like Country Joe and Ed Saunders," my wife says, as appalled as I am that Janis is crying. She goes over and puts her arms around her. "You wouldn't want to live with just one person all your life," she says, "not when you've had the opportunity to know so many. The rest of us just settle for monogamy because we're not adventurous or creative enough to figure out how else to do it."

Wait a minute, I'm thinking. Is my wife saying this because she really means it or she just wants to be consoling to Janis? Whatever her meaning, Janis is not consoled.

"I never had any kids, either," she cries. "You've got a passel of beautiful kids, too," she says to my wife.

"We've only got two, and they're not all that beautiful," my wife says.

"Well, I've got nothing," Janis cries.

I give up. This whole thing has gotten away from me. I really thought Janis would be exempt from all this shit. I know fame and fortune don't necessarily buy happiness, but don't they buy the ability to remove yourself from these situations when you don't want to deal with them anymore? Janis doesn't have to get up on stage ever again, if she doesn't want to. If she gets tired of one man, there's always another waiting in the wings. Besides, doesn't having a great voice and a great producer like me compensate for all of it? I let Janis go back to 1968. I'm not interested in what she has become. I *am* interested in what my wife had to say, however. I go up to the house, where she is canning tomatoes.

"Are you bored with me?" I ask.

She looks over at me with a frown. "What the hell brought that on?" she asks.

"Do you think life would have been more fun if you'd had a succession of partners, say, like Janis Joplin?"

"Her life's not fun at all," she says. "She's dead."

"You're right," I say, and walk back down to the pasture, where the hay grows three feet tall.

The Right Question

"Bertrand Russell asked the wrong question," Michael said to her from the overstuffed chair. "The question isn't what in life is knowable, it's what in life is worth doing."

Outside, summer had been trying to arrive for over a month, but as soon as the green shoots of grass pushed through the soil, and the forsythia burst into bloom, snow fell again.

Inside, he continued, "And the answer to my question is the same answer to Bertrand Russell's: nothing."

He had been doing plenty, really. He still got up and ran every morning, two miles up the village road to the end of the houses, past the Catholic mission church, the old school house, to Juan Valencia's fields of grazing cattle. If it took him more than half an hour to return, she knew he had been waylaid by someone along the route: the mayordomo telling him when they could take the irrigation water; a neighbor asking if he would rototill his garden plot as soon as the weather improved; Nestor, another neighbor, running alongside him to feed his horses down the road and to "give you courage to continue your run."

Back home, in their house of perpetual non-completion, he worked on any project appropriate for that day, be it plastering the mudroom, laying tongue-and-groove in the loft, or fixing the leak under the kitchen sink. For an hour found here or there, he put together his latest box, icons of his personal saints—Emily Dickinson with a sword through her heart, D. H. Lawrence with wings, Artaud with bloody hands. The gallery down the road displayed them on a wall, but no one had yet bought one to grace a home.

But he was distracted by his question, asked with increasing urgency.

"This is when your Zen training needs to come to attention," she said to him, as they bent over the rows of peas they were planting, one at a time, two inches apart. "Planting peas is what we are doing; therefore it is worth doing."

"That's my line," he said.

"That's the trouble," she said. "You're not saying it, much less doing it."

"I can't stand your fortitude," he said.

"You don't want me to get depressed too, do you? One of us at a time is enough."

"Why shouldn't you get depressed with me. There's every reason to."

It had always been a problem with them, how to react. When he was depressed she was supposed to cheer him up, but her optimism killed him. It meant she wasn't taking him seriously. When she was depressed, he teased her out of it, and she *knew* he wasn't taking her seriously.

Once the peas and lettuce and cabbages were planted and it finally stopped snowing, he was distracted by the garden and gathering wood, a chore he still loved after twenty years' necessity. The split and stacked woodpile outside the door gave him tremendous satisfaction, he said—at least they'd never freeze.

One afternoon he decided to make tamales for dinner: untraditional tamales, from a famous restaurant cookbook, with zucchini and cheese.

About three o'clock he came upstairs where she was working and said, "I give up. They're too hot—I put in only mild chile, but they're too hot— and the kids will never be able to eat them. I'm not making dinner."

"Well, Michael," she said, "it's a little late notice, but I guess I can make something. Are you sure they'd be too hot once you got them in the masa and it all mixes together in your mouth?"

"They're too hot. I can't even cook dinner."

She stopped doing what she was doing. It was obvious he needed her attention.

"Why don't you go out and chop some wood and I'll make dinner," she said.

"I don't feel like chopping wood," he said. "I don't feel like doing anything."

"You might as well do something to distract yourself."

"That's the trouble," he said. "It's all a distraction. That's why none of it is worth doing."

"Is it just what you're doing that's a distraction, or what everybody's doing?" she asked.

"I don't think you'd call what's going on in South Africa a distraction, or what Indians in Guatemala and Mexico are doing," he said.

They'd had this conversation before.

"Is that what you want to be doing?" she asked.

"It's not a question of what I want to be doing," he said, "it's a question of what I am doing, and it stinks. I'm not a South African or a Mexican or a Guatemalan, I'm a privileged white boy from the good old USA who wouldn't know how to fight a revolution if it came knocking at my own back door. I'm too busy distracting myself making crummy boxes no one wants to buy. I'm taking my boxes out of the gallery."

"Don't take it so personally," she said. "If you want to try and make a little money, leave them there. One will sell eventually. If you're not interested in making any money, take them out and we'll enjoy them here."

"Art is crap. Literature is crap. Music is the only thing that still has any purity, before the record companies get hold of it and turn it into big business."

With that he went downstairs, put on Chet Baker, and spent the rest of the afternoon on the couch.

"What's with Dad?" the kids asked when they got back later that day from visiting their grandparents. At twelve and fifteen they really didn't care all that much about their parents' moods, but they still noticed.

"He's feeling old," she said.

"He is old," said Sam, the fifteen-year old.

"You want to talk about old," said Kiko, the twelve-year old, "you should spend two weeks with Grandma and Grandpa. All they want to do is sit on the porch drinking martinis and then go out to eat."

"Don't tell me your Dad is old because I'm only a year younger than he is and I don't feel old. And if I find out you two were impolite or snotty to your grandparents you can forget about doing anything else this summer but chores," she said.

"Just kidding, Mom," Sam said. "Dad can still beat me at one-on-one."

"Why don't you ask him to play some basketball with you. He always feels better after he's creamed you," she said.

Later, while they were having a drink and she cooked dinner, Michael read her an article from the newspaper about a group back East that had taken over a stockbroker's office and made everyone dress up as feudal usurers before putting them in handmade stocks.

"At least somebody still occasionally does something that's in their faces, and creative at that," he said. "All anybody does anymore is write 'outraged' letters to the editor and file lawsuits."

"You think we'd be more politically involved than we are if we lived back there?" she asked.

"Not necessarily," he said. "But maybe we'd find some people who are a little more aware of what is really going on in this world and aren't afraid to talk about it. Living in urban areas makes it harder to ignore just how fucked up things are. "

"Can't be any of your old friends," she said. "According to you they're all yuppies now and completely apolitical. And they were at the vanguard with you in the sixties."

"Maybe there isn't anyone left," he said. "Maybe these people who took over the stock exchange are really only left over yippies and don't know any more than the rest of them."

They ate dinner outside under the ramada made of peeled aspen branches. It was a still night—the afternoon rains had yet to arrive—and the sound of the river was in their ears.

"So you boys glad to be home?" he asked the kids, as they gobbled down her chicken tacos, what she'd been able to come up with on the spur of the moment.

"Yeah, but we did some fun stuff with Grandma and Grandpa," Kiko said. "I'll tell you, though, I'm not going to eat any more red meat for a year. Grandma and Grandpa sure eat a lot of steak and stuff."

"It was great," Sam said. "Filet mignon, roast beef, leg of lamb. How come we never eat meat like that around here?"

"I don't think they eat like that when you're not there," she said. "It's just that it's easy to cook, and it's a treat for them to eat it with you. And don't exaggerate, you know we do eat red meat occasionally when someone around here butchers a cow and gives us some."

"I'll tell you why we don't buy red meat that isn't raised around here," Michael said. "Because this great country of ours is busily subsidizing South American countries that are stealing the land from their peasants and Native Americans and turning it over to corporate ranchers so they can cut down the remaining tropical forests and raise cows for McDonald's hamburgers."

"We know that, Dad," Kiko said. "There's a campaign at school to boycott McDonald's."

"Another great one issue political stand," Michael said. "Let the kids boycott McDonald's, make them feel like they're doing something worthwhile, saving the rain forests in South America, while people in their own community are malnourished and drug addicts because they don't have a job."

"You're the one who just said we don't eat meat because of what's going on in South America," Sam said indignantly. "What's your problem?"

"My problem is that there's nothing in this goddamned world worth doing because no one has any idea what's going on, much less what to do to stop it. I'm going down to the river. Maybe I'll have a real life experience with a fish."

She soon began to tire of the situation. It was nice to have the boys back, she'd missed them, but they were already complaining about the neglected chores they had to attend to. And as the days warmed up enough to set out the tomatoes and plant the corn, his mood didn't get any better. They spent three days wiring and plastering the bathroom, the last of the downstairs rooms to be finished. He worked hard, as he always took pride in his plastering skills, but this time it was without any of his usual enthusiasm and attention. They both fell into bed, exhausted, at nine o'clock. Three hours later they woke up to pounding on the front door.

"Oh shit, there's someone at the door," she said, rising up out of bed to peer out the window in an attempt to see the doorway in the pitch-black night. "Is it locked?"

"Of course not, you know we never lock the door at night," he said, getting out of bed and pulling on his sweat pants.

"It was just wishful thinking," she said, putting on her robe.

They both went downstairs and he approached the door.

"Can you see who it is?" she asked, hiding behind the huge post that divided the living room and dining room.

"I knew there would come a time we regretted not installing a porch light," he said. "We have to answer the door. Whoever is out there already knows there's somebody home. We've got to quit leaving the living room lamp on."

He opened the door and there stood a young man in a head kerchief.

"I'm really sorry, man, but I couldn't rouse no one else. I went off the road and I'm stuck in the ditch and my kids are in the car. Do you think you could pull me out with a chain or a winch or something?"

"What ditch do you mean?" Michael asked. "On this road?"

"Just up the road, man, where it curves around."

"I don't think I've got anything I can pull you out with," he said. "We just have one of those small pick-ups."

"Can you come and try, man, I can't leave my kids in the car. We were headed up the canyon where our friends are camped and I need to get the kids up there and into bed. They're just little kids. I'm really sorry man, I knocked on a bunch of doors down the road but nobody would answer."

"Just a minute, let me talk to my wife," Michael said.

"I'm really sorry, man, I know how it is to be waked up in the middle of the night."

"What am I going to do?" he whispered to her. "I can't just turn the guy away, although I'm not so sure about this."

"Well one thing for sure is you're not going out there by yourself," she whispered back. "You probably can't pull him out anyway—the truck isn't powerful enough. Why couldn't he have woken Orlando up? He has a big four-wheel drive."

"Because Orlando had enough sense not to come to the door," he said. "I don't think I have any choice but to at least go out and see if I can help the guy."

"Then I'm going with you," she said. "I'll wake up Sam and make him sit up until we get back."

"I don't think you have to come with me," he said. "I guess the guy is probably okay."

"I'm coming," she said, and went upstairs to get dressed. She shook Sam awake and whispered to him what was going on, then made him get up and follow her downstairs. She knew if she left him in bed he'd be asleep again in a minute.

"If we're not back in forty-five minutes, call the police," she whispered.

He looked shocked.

"It's just in case we can't get him out and we need some help," she reassured him. "Now don't fall asleep. And lock the door after us."

They went out to where the man was waiting in the yard.

"I'm really sorry, ma'am," he said when he saw her. "I didn't have no choice. I got kids."

"It's okay," she said. "Let's go see what we can do.

They all got into the pick-up and drove down the road to the first curve coming into the village, where anyone who was destined to go off the road always did. There was the man's car, a big old American sedan of some kind, sideways in the ditch. Michael dropped them off at the car and turned the truck around so it was in front of the car, pointing down the road. The car windows were rolled up tight but she could see someone sprawled across the front seat, and two little kids huddled in the back.

"Unlock the door, Felix," the man said, rapping on the window. The figure in the front seat didn't move.

A little boy opened one of the back doors.

"Get your brother and come out here," the man said to the boy.

Two little boys, who looked to be about six and four, climbed out the door.

"Why don't you come over and stand by me," she said.

They obediently followed her over to the other side of the road. They were shirtless and obviously very sleepy.

The man rummaged around the back seat of the car and came out with a chain.

"I got a chain, man." They knelt in front of the car to look for what they could attach the chain to. They hooked it onto the frame, and then attached the other end to the tow bar on the back of the pick-up.

"Okay, let's see how bad you're in," Michael said, getting into the truck. He put it in low four-wheel drive, and slowly applied the gas. The car jerked forward, then rolled back into place in the ditch.

"I'll get in and give her some gas," the man said, "that'll get her out." He had to push the other man out of the driver's seat to climb behind the wheel.

This time the car rocked forward, then settled back again as the spinning wheels spun rocks and debris out of the ditch.

Michael got out of the truck and surveyed the situation.

"Let's try putting something under the rear wheels to provide some traction," he said. "We should have brought some boards from the house."

They scavenged for some tree branches and wedged them cross ways underneath the wheels.

"I'll push this time," she said. "Stay here, kids, out of the way."

"Just be careful you don't get hit by flying rocks or branches," Michael said, and climbed back into the truck.

"We'll get her out this time, man," the man said.

Rocking back and forth a few times to get some momentum, Michael gunned the truck and the car skidded along the ditch a few feet, straightening out in the process.

"Let's try it again," he called from the truck.

"Wait a minute, let me move the tree branches back under the wheels," she said.

"That's okay, I think we've got it," he called.

Watching from the truck, Michael quickly applied the gas, and this time the car straightened up even more and when he hit the gas harder, it jerked up the bank of the ditch and came to rest on the road.

"All right, man," the man said, as he climbed out of the car and crawled under the car to retrieve his chain.

"You kids okay?" she asked. They didn't answer, but hurried to climb back into the car.

"Let me give you guys a beer, man," he said, throwing the chain into the car and rummaging around on the floor. "I guess we drank them all," he said, grinning. He walked up to them and gave them both the soul handshake. "Thanks, man, I really appreciate it. Some people won't help nobody these days, cause they think we're all banditos or something." Once again he pushed the man in the car back into the passenger's seat and got in the car. "I'll drop you by a six pack on my way back down," he said and started up the road, this time more slowly.

"He didn't even check to see if the kids were in the car," she said.

"I'm sure he knew they were," Michael said. "Come on, let's get home."

Sam was asleep on the couch when they walked in.

"He didn't lose any sleep worrying," he said, and poked him awake. "We're home, you can go back to bed."

"What was that all about?" Sam asked.

"We'll tell you in the morning," he said, and walked him upstairs.

"Want a drink?" she asked, upon his return.

"I want three."

She fixed their drinks and turned off all the lights before sitting down in the living room.

"No more night light, right?" she said.

"Right," he said.

Through the huge living room windows she could see the brilliant starlit sky, revealed only to those who lived far away from the lights made brilliant by man. "I hope those kids are all right. I didn't like the way he acted towards them."

"Oh, it was just late and he was hassled," he said, sipping his drink. "I'm sure they're fine with all their friends up in the campground. I'm just glad everything worked out okay. Looks like it's still all right to be a Good Samaritan sometimes."

"Only if you live up here," she said. "We'd never even consider opening our door if we lived in a city."

"We'd never make it in a city anymore," he said. "We lost our urban survival skills a long time ago." He smiled, and looked more relaxed than she'd seen him look in months.

"Feeling a little bit better about things after tonight's adventure?" she asked.

"Somewhat," he said. "I think that's what you'd call a real life experience. Something happened and I responded without too much reflection or debate. Maybe I'm still alive."

Over the next few weeks he went about his routine with more of his old enthusiasm and even started on the adobe wall they had talked about building around the ramada and flowerbeds in front of the house. She, on the other hand, somehow felt she'd taken a step backwards. Maybe it was because of all the worrying she'd been doing about him, or maybe it was the image of those two kids that she couldn't shake loose from her mind. Every day in the paper she read a story about child abuse or starving people in Somalia or thirty more people dying in South Africa and it always gave her pause, until she went on to the next article to erase the memory. This time, though, the story stayed in her head as she began harvesting the snap peas that hung from the vines in vulgar profusion.

As always, as soon as he noticed she was down, he teased and cajoled until, once again, she came around. The small lump of resentment that lived in the pit of her stomach grew a little bigger, but she really didn't have time to think about the pattern. In the long run, it didn't matter. They survived, and while it wasn't always enough, it was what you had to do.

Emergencies

He fell off the roof as they were pounding in nails, and she took him to the emergency room of the county hospital. Two men in green came out with a wheel chair and officiously rolled him in the red swinging doors, away from her, to the depths of specialization. She gave statistics at the window: age, occupation, next of kin, insurance—none. He told her later when he hit the ground the first thing he thought of was the article in the newspaper about the man who had been attacked on Central Avenue walking home from work. "I can't afford this," the man said, as the knife sliced open his back.

She sat in the waiting room, and one of the green men came out and told her that they were still cleaning up the head wound, that they would begin to stitch him up soon, that he would be fine. She thanked him and asked if she could come in. His face adopted its official feature, no, that's not allowed. So she sat outside, waiting.

Soon a woman came wandering down the hall holding a box of Ensure. She began to weave, then suddenly sat down, and sighed.

"Are you all right?" she asked the woman.

"Oh," the woman said. "I'm so dizzy. Do you have a car?"

"Yes, but I have to stay here with my husband. He fell off the roof."

"Oh, I'm so sorry," the woman said. It was really a whine, but it came from her heart. "I'm so dizzy, I can't take the bus."

"Do you have to take the bus somewhere? I'll help you get on the bus." The green man had said it would take at least an hour to stitch him up. She'd seen his skull when she found him there on the ground. She'd heard the cry and turned to see him go tumbling through the air. It had been a relief to discover she was not so far removed from her instincts as she thought—her legs had moved, her thoughts focused, her hands quickly covered the wound to stop the bleeding. Her voice soothed, reassured, disconnected from her own hysteria long enough to convince him that she would take care of him, that he would be all right.

"Oh, the bus driver, he won't let me on the bus anymore because I fell down last time and he had to stop the bus to help me," the Ensure lady said.

"Isn't there someone who could come take you home?" she asked.

"No, they're all saying rosary," the Ensure lady said. "My cousin died and I have to go to the rosary but they gave me a shot and I'm too dizzy and they won't let me on the bus."

She saw one of the emergency room staff walk by and approached her.

"This woman says she got a shot and she doesn't feel well enough to take the bus. Could you help her, please?"

The emergency room woman leaned down and asked the lady with the Ensure, "Who treated you, ma'am? Who gave you a shot?"

"I don't know," the Ensure lady said. "They gave me a shot and I feel dizzy and my cousin died and I have to go to the rosary."

Someone from the walk-in clinic came by, and the emergency room woman asked her, "Did you treat this lady today? She says she got a shot and she's dizzy."

The walk-in clinic woman looked at the Ensure lady and said, "She didn't get a shot, we took her blood."

The emergency room woman said, "You're all right, ma'am, they just took your blood. Why don't you just sit here for a few minutes until you feel better."

So the Ensure lady sat there, clicking her teeth and sighing.

"Can't you call the funeral home and have someone come pick you up?" she asked after everyone had gone away and left them.

"They're all saying rosary. They'll be there for hours. My husband, he's there too."

"Can't you call him to come get you?" she asked again.

"I come here every day and they give me a shot because I haven't eaten in eleven days and my husband makes me wait from the morning till four o'clock to come pick me up, but now he's saying rosary and no one will come pick me up and they won't let me on the bus."

"You mean to tell me your husband is at some funeral home saying rosary for some dead person, making you sit here all day waiting for him to come pick you up?" she said.

"He's sixty-five. He don't care no more."

A security guard came by with a walkie-talkie growing out of his ear. She asked him if he could give the Ensure lady a ride home because her family was all saying rosary for her cousin and no one would come get her. The security guard leaned his radio-less ear down to the Ensure lady and said, "Now what seems to be the problem?"

"My cousin died and I have to go to the rosary only they won't let me on the bus," the Ensure lady said.

"Hospital policy says no rides, ma'am," the security guard said. The walkie-talkie started buzzing in his ear.

"Can you at least take her to the bus so she can get up to the funeral home where her husband is with the car?" she asked the man, between buzzes.

"I'll see what I can do," he said, and walked off.

A different man in green came out of the emergency room and said to her, "Joe would like to see you before we start stitching him up."

She grabbed her jacket, then hesitated, looking at the Ensure lady.

"What are you going to do? I have to go into the emergency room, my husband wants me."

"You go in and take care of your husband," the Ensure lady said. "I'm going to the chapel upstairs. I guess I'll just have to wait until my husband comes for me."

"I'm sorry. I wish there was something I could do."

"You have your husband to worry about, don't you worry about me," the Ensure lady said, and started off down the hall towards the elevator. The carton of nutritional supplement stuck out from beneath her arm like a gift from Gomorrah.

She followed the green man into the emergency room, past white curtained cubicles revealing naked feet and arms and chests and thighs. In the end one, the curtain standing open, Joe lay on a stretcher, his head pointed away from her.

"Hi," he said. "I'm sorry."

"Sorry for what?" she said, taking his hand, leaning down to kiss him. As she bent over she saw his skull again, surrounded by orange, the disinfectant.

"For screwing things up so badly," he said. He was crying, so she didn't.

"Don't be ridiculous," she said. "They're going to get you all sewed up and I'll take you home, and to hell with everything else for awhile."

The green man came up and said, "We're ready to stitch him up now," and started putting on plastic gloves. She tried to read the identification card on his chest to see who he was. He looked awfully young to be a doctor.

"I want you to say with me," Joe said, holding her hand tightly.

She looked at the green man and raised her eyebrows questioningly.

"Sounds like a good idea to me," he said. "It's bending the rules a little, but I'd say this particular laceration is spectacular enough to warrant some rule bending."

She saw his name, Bob Masey, and his title, technician. She didn't know what a technician was, but she knew it wasn't a doctor. She tried to be tactful.

"So you're the one who has to sew him up?" she said, smiling.

He looked at her and smiled back.

"The doctors never do jobs like this," he said. "It takes too long. They leave it to us lackeys. On the job training, you know."

She kept smiling.

"Just kidding," he said, planting himself in a chair next to Joe's head. The other green man, watching, added, "Bob's the best we've got, really. He gets all the gory ones."

As Bob pulled each suture through Joe's scalp, puncturing the skin with the small, hooded needle tied to the thread, she kept her eyes on the technician's face, puckered in concentration. Joe's face was covered with a sterile towel, like he was dead.

Every few minutes someone in green or white came by to stare at Joe's scalp and Bob's work. "Beautiful job, Bob," they would say. "That's some laceration there." They all wore smocks or pajamas or white coats and looked very professional. They all drank cokes and talked about what they were going to do on their days off.

She saw two of the white coated ones wheel an old, yellow woman into a cubicle across the isle. They kept asking her questions, and she kept answering "Oh... Oh... Oh..." Finally they realized she spoke only Spanish. There was no one on duty who also spoke Spanish, so they borrowed the man in the next cubicle who had wandered in with two broken ribs.

"They want to know where you hurt," he said to her in Spanish. He was a neat little man with gray hair and an impeccable mustache. He looked like a doll in his blue-flowered emergency room gown.

"Oh...," she answered.

"She only says 'Oh'...," the little man said.

"Obviously," the orthopod said. That's what they kept calling him, one of the men in the white coats. He was a neat little man, too, only thirty years younger than the interpreter, and his neatness was rather insipid. "Tell her she's got a broken arm, and from her coloring and abdominal swelling, it's obvious she has some sort of tumor. Ask her if she knows she has a tumor."

"I don't know the word in Spanish for tumor," the little man said.

"How about cancer?" the orthopod asked.

The little man seemed shocked, but he leaned closely over the yellow woman and emitted a stream of Spanish.

She heard the woman answer weakly in words she couldn't quite catch, not that she would have understood them anyway. Her own Spanish was limited by the prevailing attitude that it was easier to make everyone else learn English.

"She says she's come here to die," the little man said, in a very serious tone. Despite his bruised ribs, he held himself tall and rigid. She could only catch glimpses of the old woman—yellow, stretched skin, white hair, wasted body.

"Tell her nonsense," the orthopod said. "And ask her to tell us the names of her family so that we may notify them of her condition."

The old man looked at the old woman and said, "Nonsense," and then broke into another stream of Spanish.

"She keeps saying George and Carlos and Mimi but she won't tell me who she's talking about," he said a few minutes later. "Is she really going to die?"

"Tell her we must get this arm set and then we'll admit her to the hospital," the orthopod said. He came out of the cubicle and beckoned to some women in white with a jerk of his arm. "Thank you, sir," he said to the little man, "you've been most kind."

The little man wandered back to his cubicle and lay down on his stretcher. A band of women wheeled tables full of bone setting paraphernalia next to the old woman. The orthopod went into a lengthy speech of unintelligible terms, and the curtain closed.

"How are you doing, honey?" she asked Joe, gently lifting the towel over his face for added air.

"Okay," he said.

"How are you doing?" she asked Bob, bent over his stitches.

"Who, me?" he said. "It's as easy as one, two, three." He leaned back, blinking his eyes, stretching his fingers. She saw the clock on the wall. He'd been sewing for an hour.

"I have to pee," Joe said.

"Good," Bob said. "I need a break. I finally got these vessels closed up and I can begin sewing the outer layer of the skin now. Think you can walk to the bathroom?"

"I think so," Joe said, slowly sitting up.

She put her arm under his shoulders and walked him across the hall to the toilet.

"Don't look in the mirror," she said, switching on the light. But he did.

"I've been scalped," he said, looking at the cut that ran from the bottom of his forehead across the top of his head and down towards his left ear.

"Lobotomized," she thought. She helped him find the toilet, then led him back to the stretcher where Bob sat waiting.

"I'm going to make the stitches as small as possible back into the hairline, just in case," he said.

"His father and his brother are almost bald," she said.

"Aha!" Bob said.

"I've always had a high forehead," Joe said.

Little stitches of blue slowly made their way up his forehead. She looked at the clock again; it was three hours now. All the other occupants in the cubicles had changed at least once. Bob kept stitching.

She could hear the voices from behind the white curtain next to them, a man and a woman talking.

"There's nothing physically wrong with you that we can determine," the man said.

"I'm not leaving," the woman said. "I can't go back."

"What do you mean you can't go back?" the man asked.

"My husband doesn't love me anymore, and my kids don't care. I can't go back and pretend that it's all right, because it isn't. My life is like hell."

"How did you end up here?"

"The cops picked me up in a bar and I told them I was sick."

"Are you sick?"

"I'm sick of life. I'm sick of trying to get along in this lousy world. I'm too sick to try anymore. I'm not leaving here. There's nothing to do anymore."

"Ma'am, I appreciate your problems, but you can't stay in the emergency room."

"Why do you call it an emergency room if you can't take care of people. Take care of me, please."

"Look," the man said. "I'll tell you what I'll do. I'll refer you to the mental health hospital and you can talk with someone there."

"I'm not leaving."

"I'll have someone come over here and get you. Why don't you come out to the desk with me while I call the hospital?"

She quickly looked up as the curtain opened. A man in white, with a tie and clipboard, came out of the cubicle and raised his eyebrows at Bob, who was also looking. A small, dark haired woman followed him, pushing at her hair, pulling at her sweater. Their eyes met momentarily, and she quickly lowered hers from the vulnerable ones that challenged her curiosity. She turned back to Joe and he squeezed her hand.

After four hours it was over. His head was sewed up, and they were going home. Bob pulled off his rubber gloves, threw them in the garbage, and went to get the doctor. She looked at the entire line of stitches for the first time. It looked like the embroidery she had once done on a pillow.

A man in white, the doctor, came back with Bob.

"A brilliant job," he said. "First rate. You were in good hands, young man," he said to Joe. "Lucky for you it happened tonight—one more day and Bob wouldn't have been around to give you such fine treatment."

She and Joe looked at Bob.

"They're laying me off," he said, grinning. "Not enough split heads and broken bones to keep me on. At least I'm going out in style with that head of yours."

"How unfair," she said.

"Frankly, I don't give a damn," he said. "I'm going back to school and get my nursing degree and work in obstetrics. I want to see things turn out well for awhile."

They walked back up the aisle of curtained cubicles to the desk, where they were given Joe's scissored T-shirt and a list of skull fracture symptoms, just in case. She was to wake him up every two hours to make sure he was the Joe she used to know. She heard the ambulance siren coming closer and closer, as they stood there, saying goodbye to all the men and women in green and white.

"It's the paramedic unit," one of the women in white said. "He's reported unconscious, with severe head lacerations, probable concussion with brain damage."

Everyone gathered around the red doors as the ambulance screeched to a stop. Men in blue lifted the stretcher out; clear bottles of liquid dangled like mobiles as they wheeled it in. She didn't want to look, but she did. His face was unrecognizable, covered in blood. He lay curled on his side, his legs tucked up to his belly. The doctor and the woman in white followed the men in blue into a private room and closed the door.

"He was jumped by a couple of men, and they kicked him in the head with steel-toed boots," Bob said, taking off his green smock. "All in a day's work."

She burst into tears, and Bob quickly added, "I have to goof on everything or I'd be crying, too. I'm sorry."

"That's okay," she said. "I'm sorry, too."

"Let's go home," Joe said. "It's over for us."

The Tenth Street Blues

I was reading this story by Diane di Prima the other day about sitting in an apartment in New York eating Oreos and wondering why she was getting fat. I did that, too, once, only I was in Berkeley and I knew why I was getting fat. I was depressed as hell.

I thought it would be fun living in Berkeley, in the sun, across the Bay from San Francisco, a great city. I'd go over there on weekends and ride around with my friend on his Kawasaki motorcycle and eat Chinese food. So I took this job as a teacher's aid at a private school full of professors' kids and moved into a big house on Tenth Street. A friend of mine had just moved out and warned me about the other tenants, but you couldn't beat the rent.

I lived in a room in front that used to be the living room. I bolted shut the outside door and put up a sign asking everyone to please use the back door. Out my bay window I could watch all the punks and rip-off artists who frequented the neighborhood.

I guess they figured we didn't have anything worth stealing. Except for a couple of pounds of grass Bruce had hidden in his room, they figured right. I don't know why Bruce thought he had to hide it, as no one could have gotten into his room to get it. When he was home he barred the doorway with his dresser. A double lock kept anyone out while he was away. He had a refrigerator and a hot plate in the room, and I think he urinated out the window, so you might say he had his own spaceship earth right there.

I think he was mostly trying to avoid the two gay men who lived in the attic. You know what they say that indicates. But I wasn't interested in his sexual proclivities. Chauvinist pigs don't turn me on, although occasionally their charm momentarily disarms me. Luckily my suspicious and paranoid nature surfaces quickly enough to save me undue embarrassment. Bruce's girlfriend, who lived in Fort Bragg and came to visit every weekend, was his "chick"; the women he brought home during the week his "pieces of ass." I don't know how he classified me. Sometimes he came to my room to share a joint or loan me the next installment of Don Juan, but he never made a pass. He was a jerk.

A sweet young thing from Kansas rounded out the tenancy. She lived in a bedroom off the dining room with whomever she picked up off Telegraph Ave. the night before. Sometimes she picked up so many I stumbled over them on the dining room floor in the morning on my way to the kitchen. She sold paper flowers up on campus next to the Hare Krishnas and Jesus freaks. Her Midwestern background gave her a gentle, if vacuous, nature.

The first day I went to work half the teachers were outside picketing. One of them, the sloppy liberal type with baggy pants and a bushy mustache, told me that they'd gone on strike because the director was a fascist.

"Just because we don't have a union to represent us doesn't mean we will allow demagoguery to triumph in the classroom," he said. "We are not afraid to expose a tyrant, whatever cries of sexism and racism are hurled as a paranoid defense."

He was referring to the fact that the director was a black woman. But here was a dilemma. I never crossed picket lines. I'd found that the safest position to take, regardless of what was being picketed or what dirty union was doing the picketing. This was 1971 and if I wasn't actively tearing down institutions and conspiring to overthrow the government, the least I could do was remain on the revolutionary side. They were right, after all.

"This is a real problem for me," I told him. "I just moved to town and I really need this job."

"You think we all don't need jobs?" he demanded. "I've got five kids at home, hungry, and in need of shoes, but they know their father will not betray his principles and they are proud of him for it."

"I see," I said. "Well, I guess I'll just go in and tell the director I won't be able to work until this strike is resolved."

"She knows our demands, but you can tell her for me that until she releases her stranglehold on this school we will never bless these walls with the sound of enlightened teaching."

"Okay," I said, and walked in.

"You sure picked a good time to come to work," Martha said to me, sitting in her office, the curtains closed.

"You sure got a mess on your hands out there," I said.

I'd known Martha since I was a kid. She and my mom had both worked at the City of Paris over in San Francisco years ago when they'd been career girls. Martha had progressed from sales to management to the corporate guilt syndrome alleviated by a PhD in education. My mother had progressed to a miserable marriage. I wouldn't have been able to tell you which was worse. I just wanted to take drugs and have sex and ride around on Kawasaki motorcycles.

"I try to get rid of some lousy teachers and this is what I get," Martha said. "Somehow I seem to have ended up on the wrong side of the battle again."

"How many kids are left?"

"Oh, most of them. The parents who aren't into reading and writing as part of the curriculum joined the picket line, but it's just as well. Their kids are into schizophrenia."

"So this isn't going to destroy the school like that guy out there said?"

"Legally they don't have a leg to stand on," Martha said. "I can hire and fire whomever I please."

"But it's no fun being the boss, huh?"

"You ain't kidding. How's your mom?"

"She's fine. She's thinking of coming out to visit after I get settled."

"I'd love to see her. We can reminisce about the carefree days of youth."

"I don't think they're so carefree," I said. "I have to decide whether to cross a picket line."

"I'm sorry, my dear. Older people have conveniently short memories. Your mother and I had our problems, too. Like finding a man and a career that wouldn't bum you out for the rest of your life. Why don't you go home and come back tomorrow after I threaten these assholes with criminal trespass and they slither away."

"Okay," I said. "I think I'll go out the back way and take a walk up towards campus. See the sights."

"Have a good time, dear. I'd go with you if I weren't afraid of getting stoned."

I was taking the risk of getting tear-gassed, but it was all in the day of a life, as the Beatles were saying. Maybe someone would be barricading Livermore Laboratory, decrying nuclear weapons as the tool of total destruction, or making a human chain in front of the ROTC building chanting to the cadets that they were merely fodder in the game of U.S. imperialism.

Even on the Berkeley High School campus, where I cut through to Evans Street, there were signs of revolutionary fervor: "Off the Pigs;" "Power to the People;" "Nixon sucks." My housemate Bruce was a teacher here. Women were yet to find a voice to free their chains, if he was any indication of just how far the revolution extended. I couldn't help staring at all the students as I passed by. They were all beautiful in their glow of indignation—bushy haired young men with piercing blue eyes; pig-tailed, rosy cheeked young women in sneakers and fatigues. When I was in high school the only furor generated was whether one could smoke cigarettes in the parking lot. I truly regretted the years between thirteen and eighteen, the formative years of a sniveling, self-involved personality. Ah, to be sixteen, attending SDS meetings, fucking my boyfriend in my English teacher's apartment.

I walked up past the free clinic where I'd gone after Eddie told me he had V.D. I'd stayed with Eddie and his wife Jacqueline when I'd first moved to Berkeley, before I found my house. Jacqueline had just had a baby, and Eddie told me since she couldn't have sex for six weeks they'd decided that if it was okay by me Eddie should relieve his sexual tensions in my bed. I thought this was a very liberated attitude on Jacqueline's part, and I figured I was the safest person to satisfy the sex and sanctify the family. Obviously, I wasn't the only one with whom he was finding relief, so I told Jacqueline and quickly moved into my house. Eddie came by one night to complain that the baby was keeping him awake and he needed a good night's sleep, so I offered him my couch, but I guess that wasn't what he had in mind.

Up on campus small groups of people were clustered around the various entertainers of one sort or another: musicians and singers, chanters and dancers, lecturers and haranguers. The Hare Krishnas mostly attracted each other; the largest group of folks was listening to a black woman and bearded white man play the guitar and banjo and sing. A dog with a hat hanging from its mouth made the rounds through the crowd collecting nickels and dimes.

I saw Michael and Steven, the two men who lived in the attic, standing in the crowd. I went over. I always felt like a fat slob standing next to them, and vowed to kick the Oreo habit once again. Their skinniness had to be accounted for by more than bad eating habits. Actually, whenever I saw them in the kitchen they were always frying eggs to put in a sandwich of toast with the center cut out so they could smash the yoke and it would ooze onto the honey covered bread. I think the rest of the time they stayed up in the attic, took speed, and "rapped." They were from Michigan and talked like they had a nose full of cotton.

"Howdy," I said. "What are you two doing on campus? Considering becoming academics?"

"Hell no," said Michael, the dark haired one. In the bright light of the Berkeley sun he looked like curdled vanilla pudding. "College is for good little boys and girls who want to please their parents and spend all their money."

"My mom always wanted me to be a pharmacologist," Steven said. "Then I could take care of her when she got old and sick and needed pills." Steven was blond and soft and handsome despite his pageboy haircut and size seven jeans.

"Don't worry about your mother, Steven," Michael said. "We can get all the pills we need for all her ills and everyone else's. We'll panacea the populace with Valium and Darvon so none of us feel a thing."

"Don't let the campus SDS'ers hear you say that," I said. "They hate drug crazed hippies more than bourgeois pigs."

"They're all assholes," Michael said. "Their revolutionary games are all self-indulgent middle class crap. Make 'em all go work in a Pontiac factory and see how much compassion they have for the proletariat. Turn my father loose on them for a few minutes and see if they still want to save the worker."

"See you guys later," I said.

I listened to the music awhile, ate a pretzel, and bought the *Berkeley Barb*. There, on the front page, was a picture of Dominick ______________, or Dominick the Red, as we called him. I'd gone to college with him. The article said he'd jumped bail in Boston, where he was wanted for inciting a riot, and had turned up on the streets of Berkeley where he'd been caught passing a fake credit card. Seems he had wrestled the cop to the ground, tied him up, and once more fled into the night. The whole Berkeley police force and local FBI were hunting him down.

This was especially interesting to me, not only because I'd known him at school but because he'd lived in my room on Tenth Street only a year ago. The house had seen many of us Carrington College expatriates, passing on a cheap pad to each other as we made our way in and out of Berkeley. This guy is in big trouble, I thought. I hope he's long gone to Mexico, or maybe on his way to Switzerland, where his wealthy father sat watch over his bank accounts.

I walked back down to University Ave. and hitched home. I always waited to stick out my thumb until I saw a woman in the approaching car.

They were hard to distinguish in these days of androgyny. I'd quit riding with men after the fat one in the Oldsmobile exposed his penis and asked me if it made me feel good.

When I went to work the next morning there were no picketers outside.

"It worked," I said to Martha.

"Sure," she said. "I wouldn't go to jail over this lousy job, either. Why don't you give Willie a hand with her eight-to-ten-year-olds. I've got to spend the day harassing all the parents who are left to pay up their delinquent tuitions so we can keep this place afloat. God knows why I want to."

I went into a long room filled with plastic beanbag furniture stuffed with kids. A woman in short shorts and halter-top, a scarf wrapped around her head, was on her knees administering first aid to a little kid with the beginnings of a black eye.

"What happened?" I asked.

"The kids are learning the stages of aggression," she said. "Behavior modification comes after black eyes."

"What happened to the kid who gave him the black eye?" I asked.

"He's out guilt tripping in the playground. We need to find him so Joey can hit him back and rid him of his guilt. I take it you're the new aid. Why don't you go find Aaron and bring him inside."

"Okay," I said. I had no intention of finding Aaron so Joey could punch him back, so I didn't bother asking what he looked like. I found physical violence abhorrent—another reason why I hadn't joined the Revolution. I figured a little guilt tripping was justified. My mother was an expert at laying it on me, and look what moral consciousness I had developed.

I saw a freckle-faced kid on the swings. When I got nearer I could hear him singing, "Hey, Jude."

"Are you in Willie's class?" I asked.

He immediately switched to "Eleanor Rigby."

"Is your name Aaron? Don't worry, I'm not going to make you go inside to be punched."

He sang louder and swung higher.

I looked in on the kindergarten, where the kids were dismembering stuffed animals, wandered around the playground for a while, and finally went back to Willie's class. Joey was sitting next to a dark haired kid with glasses, playing with Legos.

"I never found him," I said to Willie.

"Oh, he came back in by himself, but Joey refused to hit a kid with glasses. Joey must learn to find ways to assert himself without bowing to conventional behavior."

"Who's the kid in the swings singing Beatle songs?" I asked.

"That's John," Willie said.

"Why is he out there by himself?"

"I don't have time to deal with schizophrenics," Willie said. "I've got enough to do balancing the neurotic behavior of everyone else."

I went into Martha's office and told her I preferred working with the kindergarten kids, if they needed me.

"Willie can be a little hard to take sometimes, I know," Martha said. "But her class is the only one of the bunch that's reading and doing math at the right level. And that's what it's about, right?"

"What about the kid on the swing?" I asked.

"What?" Martha said.

"Forget it," I said. "I'll go make myself useful."

I came home with a splitting headache, ate half a package of Oreos for dinner, and retired to my room. As I was smoking a joint, someone knocked on the door.

"Go around to the back, can't you read the sign," I yelled.

They knocked again.

I put my roach in the ashtray and unlocked the door. Two men in suits stepped into my room, extending their wallets for me to read their badges. Behind them, a uniformed cop blocked the doorway with a rifle across his chest. My stomach hit my toes.

"We're from the FBI and we'd like to ask you a few questions about Dominick ______________," one of them said. "I understand he used to live in this house."

"That was more than a year ago," I said, trying to stand in front of my ashtray. "I've only lived here a week."

"Do you know the subject in question?" the other one asked.

I should never admit I even know who he is, I thought to myself. But they probably already know we'd gone to the same college and they'd know I was lying, I thought again. How do all those suspects in detective novels keep their stories straight on five seconds' notice?

"I went to the same college he did, and I knew who he was," I answered.

"You know that he was caught in Berkeley yesterday trying to use a stolen credit card?" the first one said.

"No, sir, I don't," I lied.

"You don't read the papers?" the second one asked.

"No, sir, not if I can help it," I said.

"Hippies figure it's easier to fuck the system by staying ignorant," the first one said to his partner. Then to me, very politely, requested, "We'd like to talk with the rest of the people in the house."

"I don't know who else is here," I said, stalling.

"You all do your own thing, huh?" the first one said. "We'll leave our friend Sgt. Conners here at the front door while you introduce us to your roommates. And don't worry," he said, looking at the ashtray, "we're looking for bodies, not dope."

Linda was sitting at the kitchen table eating a sandwich, and Jimi Hendrix blared from Bruce's room. I pounded on his door.

"Go away," he yelled.

"I think you better come out here, Bruce," I yelled back.

"What?" he yelled again.

"I think you'd better come out here and talk to the cops in the kitchen," I screamed.

One of the agents tried to open the door.

"He keeps it locked," I said. "He doesn't like to be bothered."

"Is that so," the agent said, squaring off his shoulders, getting ready to attack.

The music stopped suddenly and the dead bolts on the door slid open. Bruce quickly appeared.

"What's going on here?" he demanded.

The agents showed him their badges.

"We're looking for Dominick ________________," the second one said. "We know he used to live here."

"That was before my time, man," Bruce said, stepping into the kitchen, closing his bedroom door. "I read about him in the paper today. He's one crazy dude to tangle with Sheriff ______________. All Berkeley stays out of his way."

"We thought Mr. ______________ might be looking for a place to hide and show up at his former domicile," the second one said. "I take it no one here has seen anything of him?"

"He'd have to be pretty stupid to come here," Bruce said. "And from what I read in the papers Dominick the Red ain't dumb. He's managed to elude every law enforcement agency in the country."

"It's just a matter of time," the first agent said. "He'll run until he gets tired and makes a mistake and we'll get him."

"Is that what you're saying about Bernardine Dohrn and Jeff Jones?" Bruce asked. "How many years will they be on the FBI most wanted list?"

From behind the agents' backs I pulled my finger across my throat. Can it, Bruce. You don't tangle with the FBI with two pounds of pot in your room.

"By the way, gentlemen," Bruce said. "Do you have a search warrant?"

"Do you see anyone searching for anything, Dusty?" the first one said to his partner. "Seems to me we're just asking a few simple questions in a nice friendly manner."

"Well, the dude ain't here and I think unless you have a warrant you'd better leave," Bruce said.

"What about this quiet young lady here," the first one said, looking at the dumbstruck Linda.

"She wouldn't know a revolutionary if he autographed a copy of Das Kapital for her," Bruce said. "Besides, she's a transient. She's only been here a month."

"I sell flowers up on Telegraph," she said.

"Do you know a man named Dominick _________________?" the one called Dusty asked. "Where were you on Telegraph day before yesterday at noon?"

"I wasn't there at noon," she said. "I was getting my aura balanced down on Shattuck."

"Is that so," said the first one, looking her up and down. "You don't look to me like you need any balancing. Well, folks, that about wraps things up. I'm sure that if Mr. ______________ shows up you'll notify us right away, as none of you would want to harbor a fugitive, now would you?"

Nobody said anything.

The two agents turned to go.

"And if I were you," the first one said, looking at Bruce, "I'd get rid of the dope. Next time we pay you a visit we might not be in such a good mood and decide to compensate ourselves for not finding any bodies with a good bust."

They walked through the living room, across my room, and out the door. The uniformed cop tipped his hat and closed the door."

"Jesus, what assholes," Bruce said. "They couldn't even find the faggots upstairs, much less Dominick the Red. I hate pigs. They're so stupid it makes their Gestapo-type behavior all the scarier. So you went to school with this Dominick the Red dude?"

"Yeah, he was there a year before he got busted at the antiwar demonstration in Boston. He and his sister are from some wealthy European family, so I bet he's long gone by now."

"Those guys sure were creepy," Linda said.

Michael and Steven suddenly appeared from the attic. Their eyes looked like an all night battle with the speed demon.

"Did you know we were just surrounded by fifty shotgun toting pigs?" Michael yelled. "What the hell is going on here?"

"What?" I demanded.

"Oh, man, they gotta get fifty pigs together to track down one lousy revolutionary, that's too much!" Bruce said, slapping his thighs and pulling his hair. "I gotta get out of this place."

"Are they gone?" I asked.

"God, I hope so," Steven said. "Maybe they're still hiding in the bushes. We watched from the window upstairs. Who is this revolutionary you're talking about? Michael, let's go back upstairs."

"His name is Dominick the Red and he used to live here," I said. "He tied up Sheriff ___________ up on Telegraph two days ago and apparently has the whole Bay area police force out after him."

"Hah, hah, tied up Sheriff _____________," Michael giggled. "That's a riot. Then, suddenly very seriously, "Did they take the dope?"

"Nope," I said, "but they said they might be back, and they, quote, wouldn't be so nice about it, unquote."

"We're barricading the attic," Michael said. "They ain't getting a thing. If they want revolutionaries, they came to the wrong place. Long live getting high!" They turned back and retreated upstairs.

The cops never did come back, and I heard through the grapevine that

Dominick the Red was in Germany with the Red Brigade. John continued to sit in the swing singing Beatle songs until the school closed for good in the spring. Bruce moved into an apartment with one of his former high school students, poor thing, and Michael and Steven took over his room. They used the attic for séances. I eventually gave up Oreos and went back to school to please my mother. I don't know what happened to Linda; maybe she's still up on Telegraph Ave. selling her carnations and roses to the preppies I hear have taken over the campus. Although I'm no preppie, I wouldn't go back to those Tenth Street days for anything. Maybe I'm better equipped to fend off Oreo binges, but I wouldn't want to put myself to the test.

Will the Real Mayordomo Please Stand Up

Albert called late one afternoon and quickly dispensed with the social chitchat.

"Miguel's been taking all the water and says he's not going to send a peón to clean the ditch because he's the mayordomo."

"He's not the mayordomo, you are," Ben said. "He knows we just made him mayordomo on paper because you don't own any land and can't officially be the mayordomo even if you really are because you do the job."

"Then you tell him that. He won't listen to me."

Miguel is Albert's uncle and he knows that Albert is the mayordomo, the one who directs the rotation of water among the irrigators in the village. Miguel was the mayordomo for twenty years until Victor, Albert's father, took over the responsibility. Then Victor lost his arm in a tractor accident and it says in the bylaws of the acequia association that the mayordomo can't be someone who has a disability and Alberto was the only one left to do the job. But Victor hadn't put any of the land in Albert's name and neither can you be a mayordomo if you aren't a landowner. Ben was already a commissioner—treasurer and secretary of the acequia—so the only one left was Albert (Victor could be a commissioner, as that didn't require having two arms). The rest of the village irrigators, or parciantes, never came to the meetings and were happy to leave the administration of the acequia to those who had governed it for years, even if one was a gringo, Victor had only one arm, and Alberto didn't own any land.

"I'm quitting if Miguel doesn't agree to send a peon to clean the ditch and pay him the \$64 just like everyone else has to," Albert said. From the tone of his voice Ben could tell he was offended that his uncle wasn't acknowledging his status as mayordomo.

"Okay, I'll go talk to him, but we're going to go get your Dad, too, who's probably the only one Miguel's going to listen to. If he gives us any trouble we'll just tell him that the commissioners have decided he's not going to be the mayordomo, even if it's only on paper. We'll use someone else's name to make it legal and you'll continue to be the mayordomo."

"He's loco," Albert said. "And he's my uncle!"

"That's never made any difference in this crazy place."

Victor had plenty to say about it, too.

"These guys don't know nothing about how to run the ditch. That's why I don't put the land in Albert's name. You can't just decide to be the mayordomo, you've got to learn how to be the mayordomo."

"That's what we're trying to do here, Victor," Ben said. "But we had to put Miguel down as mayordomo because the land is in your name and that's what's got us into this mess."

"Albert's going to get it all when I croak so he can quit worrying and start being the mayordomo. Miguel knows he's not the mayordomo, he's just messing with you."

"It's Albert he's messing with, and apparently Albert believes him."

"Miguel can't be the mayordomo anyway. He can't walk any better than I can shovel."

"We need to go talk to him," Ben said.

"Okay, okay, vecino," he grinned.

"Bueno, amigo."

So the next morning Ben walked down the road to Miguel's house while Victor rode his four-wheeler. There was no answer at the house so they went down to his son Jimmy's house and there he was, sitting outside in the sun watching Jimmy work on one of his cars. Jimmy had a job at Los Alamos National Laboratory as an electrician and never worked the land. Miguel irrigated it all and ran a small herd of cows, like he always had, although the only way he could get around anymore was also on an ATV that he called his caballo.

"Hola, vecino," Ben said. "Cómo está?"

"Bien, bien," Miguel said, giving Ben one of those gentle handshakes that are typical of the viejos of the villages of northern New Mexico.

Ben sat down on the bench next to him, out of the wind, and made small talk with him and Jimmy for a few minutes until he thought it was time to talk about why they were there.

"So, Albert called up yesterday and says that you told him you weren't going to send a peón to clean the ditch. He says you told him you're still the mayordomo. You remember at the meeting we just put your name down as mayordomo for the record because Albert doesn't own any land, but that he's going to do the job, right?"

Miguel threw back his head and laughed and laughed.

"I really got him good, didn't I?" he said.

"You mean you were just joking with him?" Ben asked. "I think Albert believed everything you said."

"He don't know shit about being mayordomo, pero, if you say he's the mayordomo then I guess I have to send a peón to clean the ditch. I already asked someone anyway."

Ben just laughed. Apparently these guys joked with each other as much as they joked with him, to the point where he never knew when they were telling the truth or not. But asking Miguel about taking all the water was trickier. He had a reputation for hogging the water when he was mayordomo and Ben didn't doubt for one minute that Albert was right in that regard. Victor had no qualms about confronting him.

"You hogging the water again, hermano? We gotta reset the schedule after Saturday but seems like it should be coming down by now, qué no?"

"It's coming down, it's coming down, what's your hurry. Everyone's always asking, where's the water when they know it's got to go all the way up before it comes down."

Miguel was referring to the water rotation that started at the lower end of the valley, where each parciante took his or her turn watering according to how much land he or she owned. If you had a few acres then you had one water right and you got the water for 24 hours, in a good year of sufficient water, and if you had a bunch of land you had several water rights and got the water 24 hours for each right. So in order to calculate when you were due to get the water you had to know how many water rights each parciante had and how long it would take the water to move up the village until everyone had had his or her turn and then the rotation started all over again. Even the commissioners just let the mayordomo work it out and let them know when it was their turn. But when the mayordomo was taking the water out of turn it was a problem.

"Are you irrigating your fields up above?" Ben asked. "I didn't see any water coming through your compuerta at the house."

"Sí, sí, I have the water until tonight at six and then I let it go. That's the way we do it, and Albert should just quit bitching about it and wait his turn."

"He says that somehow things have gotten out of rotation and it should already be coming down," Ben said.

Miguel laughed again. "He'll never be a real mayordomo, he just wants to make trouble. He'll get his water tonight, no problem."

They decided to leave it at that, a fairly satisfactory resolution of the problem. Which was highly unusual. When it came to dealing with the acequia, solutions were few and far between. When someone wasn't complaining about the water being taken out of turn they were complaining about someone taking it too soon. Or someone not closing his or her compuerta, the gate that allowed the water to flow from the acequia madre into the landowner's field. Or not leaving enough water in the ditch so animals downstream could drink. Or not paying ditch fees. Or letting the water run down the road instead of in the field. And the ones they usually complained to were the commissioners, meaning Ben and Victor.

When Ben called Albert to tell him what Miguel had said, he answered, "He didn't sound like he was joking to me. We'll see if someone shows up to dig for him on Saturday."

Miguel's grandson showed up to dig for him on Saturday, and Miguel showed up as well, to keep an eye on things. It took Albert half an hour to figure out who was digging whose derecho, or water right, as most of the landowners in the village hired peones to clean the ditch for them. They were either too busy to do it themselves, too old, didn't live in the village anymore, or uninterested in having anything to do with the acequia. If you had more than one water right your worker had to clean a longer section than the worker digging one right. Albert was the man who laid out the sections, approved the work, and moved us up the ditch, all day long, with an hour off for lunch. By the time they reached the presa, or dam, at the river, the ditch had been cleaned of weeds, roots, garbage, and mud. When the water was released from the presa at the end of the day, it hurried down the ditch on its long journey back to the river, and ultimately, the Rio Grande.

Miguel met them the presa at five o'clock on his caballo.

"How do you like the new mayordomo?" he asked Ben, as he lay on the ditch bank, resting.

"Albert did a good job, and he's not as mean as you," Ben said.

"You got to be mean to get these pendejos to do any work. I bet there's still jaras all along the ditch that you guys didn't cut," Miguel said.

"We cut all the jaras," Ben said. "And they were a real mess, believe me."

"That's cuz you got to cut them every year and not let them get too big and suck up all the water."

"Well, vecino, we cut them every year when Victor was the mayordomo, just like we cut them every year when you were the mayordomo. So what do you think about that?" Ben laughed.

"I think you're all loco, that's what I think, and I'm glad I'm not the mayordomo anymore," Miguel said.

Just then Albert opened the presa so the water could flow down the newly cleaned acequia.

Miguel got back on his caballo and took off down the road.

"I bet that old son of a gun is going to go open his compuerta and take the water before anyone else, to hell with the rotation," Albert said disgustedly.

"Oh well," Ben said. "For now, there's enough water for everyone. Just go close his compuerta at six tonight and start the regular rotation. If he complains tell him to talk to us about it."

Albert shrugged his shoulders and went off to pay the peones who had worked all day on the ditch.

Ben and Victor looked at each other and laughed. Not too bad for a day's work.

Life's Other Side

The only ones who ever pick you up are the ones from "life's other side." That's what Hank Williams calls them in a song, the ones who drive '65 Chevies with broken windshields and heaters that don't work. Even though Hank Williams drove Cadillacs and tipped with twenty-dollar bills I think he probably thought he belonged to the world of whores and gamblers and "heartbroken mothers and children." He was an alcoholic at fourteen and died with a dose of morphine at twenty-nine.

The car dies at the "Scenic View" pullover at Laguna. That's an Indian pueblo on Route 66, halfway between Albuquerque and Grants, New Mexico, where tourists stop and take pictures of the white mission church on the hill, surrounded by mud houses. It really is a beautiful sight, with snow-covered mountains as a backdrop, but I am in no mood for scenery. Cars are the curse of the world, I guess. I once knew a man who worked for days and days on his pick-up, getting it all fixed up and running smooth until one day he was a block from his house and it threw a rod. He got out of the pick-up, walked to his house, got his rifle and shot his truck through the heart.

I've owned cars for twenty years and I still don't understand a damn thing about them. That's like eating Danish pastry for breakfast every morning and wondering why you're fat. So when this one starts coughing and belching up the hill to Laguna I know it's going to be a long day. I take a cursory look under the hood, pull a wire and jab at a screw, but since I don't know the distributor from the alternator, my inspection is strictly for show. I soon put my pack on my back, take my dog in my arms, and walk over to the eastbound lane going towards Albuquerque.

The temperature is about twenty degrees, but the New Mexico sun shines clear and bright. It gives the desert landscape a precision the internal combustion engine will never know. We walk alongside the road to keep warm.

About ten minutes later an old Ford pick-up pulls over. I put my pack and my dog in the back, and climb into the cab.

"How far are you going?" I ask the dark, curly-haired man driving.

"You know Peña Roja? My father, he's got a ranch at Peña Roja," the man says.

"So your father has a ranch. You work on the ranch?" I ask.

"Nah," he says, waving out at the desert. "I never was a good rancher. If I had all those cows I'd probably butcher them all and eat them."

I laugh. "Thanks for picking me up."

"Yeah, man, it's cold as a witch's tit out there. You see the fight last night?"

"No, I didn't. Who won? Sugar Ray Leonard?"

"Yeah, that Sugar Ray knocked that Mexican cold. It was a good fight. My brother and me watched it at the Kitchen. You know that bar out in Grants?"

"No, I've never been there."

"It's a wild place, that bar, lots of miners drinking and throwing their money around. I was working out at the mine at Seboyeta. You know Seboyeta? But they laid me off so now I got to go to Albuquerque to get me a job. This time I'm getting an inside job. It's too cold to bust my ass outside."

"How come they laid you off?" I ask. "I thought the uranium mining around here was really going strong."

"Oh, you know how those bosses are, man. They give you a taste of that good stuff, then they throw you away. Keep 'em moving. Less trouble like that." He reaches under the seat and pulls out a beer. "My brother, he tried to make me eat this morning, but I got so drunk last night I got to keep drinking so I don't give no hangover time to catch me. I smoked a joint, too. That keeps the headache away."

"For a while," I laugh.

He puts the beer up to his mouth, but nothing comes out.

"Frozen," he laughs. He sets his beer on the dashboard to thaw out in the sun. "You know what happened last night, these guys left the bar with this woman who was pretty drunk and I think they treated her pretty bad."

"There's too much of that kind of thing going on," I say. "I don't like it."

"I don't either, man," he says. "I know where those guys live and I got me a good rifle."

We ride along in silence for a while. I look back at my dog and she's barking her head off. I think she heard our conversation.

He points out across the desert to the east.

"You know that little town Dolores? That's where I got to turn off to my father's ranch."

"That's fine," I say. "If you could just let me off before the exit, I'm sure I can catch another ride to Albuquerque."

"Sorry I can't take you all the way there but my old man's got to get a couple of days work out of me sometimes. He's getting old and don't chase those cows so good anymore. You could come with me but they shoot strangers in Peña Roja." He looked across at me for a reaction and then breaks into a huge smile. "They shoot at me, too, sometimes, but they never hit me."

"Thanks for the ride, man," I say, jumping out and whistling for my dog.

"No problem," he says. "Maybe I'll pick you up again sometime."

It's warmed up a little, so we stand by the road watching the cars go by. There are basically three categories of travelers, from the hitchhiker's point of view. First of all, there are the people in the Mercedes Benzes. Now, I heard on TV the other day that a Mercedes Benz sells for $50,000 and gets sixteen miles to the gallon. So when the people driving these cars pass me by I have to assume they don't even see me. I mean they aren't even aware of my corporeal body. Money does that, you know. It makes it possible to see only what you want to see, like $50,000 cars and $400,000 houses and people who think and act just like you do. Hitchhikers aren't even in their vocabulary.

When I see a Mercedes Benz pass by (this includes Lincoln Continentals as well; Cadillacs are sometimes excepted, as occasionally you run across someone from life's other side, like Hank Williams, who has unexpectedly come into some money and blows it on a Cadillac without ever leaving the ranks from which he came), I don't even hold out my thumb. Sometimes I salute, though. It's the only fitting thing to do.

The second type are the ones in the new Nissans and Volvos who look at you and shrug their shoulders or wave, meaning, I'd like to pick you up, buddy, but you know how it is, all those stories about hitchhikers, I've got a wife and kids and can't take any chances. They still see you but their vision is getting blurry. I usually turn around to stare at them with disgust as they drive by. I figure they're still receptive to guilt.

My first ride and the car that is just pulling over now represent the third kind. It looks like a '70s' Chevy, and by the way it's hugging the ground, carrying a big load. Before I can get to where it's stopped, a man gets out of the driver's side. He's wearing cowboy boots and aviator sunglasses; red hair and wrinkles go along with the look.

"I hate seeing anybody stuck out on the highway—been there myself a few times," he calls to me as he throws open his trunk and starts hauling suitcases and sleeping bags out of the backseat and cramming them in. A young man gets out of the passenger's seat and grins shyly at me.

"Thanks for stopping. My car broke down and I have to get to Albuquerque," I say. "Hope you don't mind the dog—she's well behaved."

"Why would I mind a dog?" the man says. "I love animals."

So we cram ourselves into the back seat. My dog is sitting on a suitcase, and I'm in between two cases of Coors. I noticed when I got in that the license plate said California.

"You coming all the way from California?" I ask.

The man laughs. "Further than that—Idaho. California's where my first car died and where I bought this heap that gets about 16 miles to the gallon." He turns around and extends his hand. "My name's Paul Watkins."

"James Ellery," I say. "Please to meet you."

The kid turns quickly around and says, "I'm Skeeter."

He's wearing a crocheted hat and three sweaters; the fuzz is just beginning to show on his upper lip. He smokes Camels and Paul smokes Salems.

"No," Paul continues, "I've had it with the Northwest. I lived all around up there, Idaho and Eugene, Oregon and Eureka, California, and it's time to go back to Oklahoma. I'm an Okie and always will be, I guess."

"I used to live in California," I say. "A place called Healdsburg, just north of Santa Rosa. I got tired of it, too."

"Oh, yeah," Skeeter says. "I'm from Ukiah."

"Oh, yeah," I say. "I know where that is. Where you headed?"

"Florida."

"What part of Florida?"

"Sarasota. My uncle's got a resort there and I'm going to cook for him."

"That sounds pretty good. At least it's warm there. This New Mexico desert gets pretty cold in the winter. But it's better than California. I heard a good joke the other day. How many Californians does it take to screw in a light bulb?"

"How many?" Skeeter asks.

"Five," I say. "One to screw in the bulb and four to share in the experience."

"Hey, that's good," Paul laughs. "I guess those folks in California figure they got to do all the experiencing they can before they fall off into the ocean."

"Ukiah's okay," Skeeter says, studying the map. "What are those mountains up there?"

"Those are the Sandias, right outside of Albuquerque," I answer.

"They look pretty high," Skeeter says. "I bet it takes some hard hiking to get to the top."

"Sandia Crest is almost 11,000 feet," I say. "They have a foot race up there every summer, seven and a half miles up a trail to the Crest. I'll bet you can't guess what the record is. A Jemez Indian ran it last year in fifty-eight minutes. Seven and a half miles in fifty-eight minutes. Pretty incredible, huh?"

"Gee whiz," Skeeter says. "I would've liked to see that."

"I saw him cross the finish line," I say. "He wasn't even breathing hard."

"An Indian, you say," Paul says, reaching under the seat for a pint of vodka. He takes a long swig and offers it to me. "I guess the white man's booze hasn't killed all of them yet. You know about the Indians out in Oklahoma, don't you? They shoved them onto this piss-poor, wind-blasted hellhole of a reservation to rot and they up and discovered oil and became millionaires. You can bet those white folks are shitting in their pants over that one."

"The Indians around here aren't so rich," I say. "Neither are many of the rest of us, for that matter."

"New Mexicans and Okies must be pretty much alike, I figure," Paul says. "Lots of sand and no trees makes life kinda like the worm in the bottom of the mescal. Makes you wonder why I'm going back after twenty years, but I'm tired of living where the sun never shines, and I got nothing holding me there anyway. My uncle wrote me a letter and wanted me to come back to Oklahoma to help him out. My aunt just died of lung cancer, and their son, my cousin, is in the army somewhere out there in the Middle East. My uncle's got a farm on some more of that wind blasted Okie soil, only there ain't no oil under his. So I told him I'd come help him out. There's nobody left but me and him.

"Here I am going back home to be a farmer after twenty years of doing just about anything to keep from being a farmer—driving trucks, cutting trees, washing dishes, picking grapes. Now that's the closest thing I did to farming, and I only did that for two weeks when I was hiding out from the cops my wife had on my tail for not paying child support. My ex-wife, I should say. I would have been glad to pay child support if she would have paid me some support for stealing my spirit. That woman knew how to kick a man when he was down, let me tell you. She was running around earning all kinds of money with this little subpoena business she got going for herself, tracking down these witnesses to go and squeal on somebody in court. So she doesn't need my money anymore until I up and leave her and put a dent in her pride, showing the world she can't keep a man. Now she says I got to send her money every month for the kid. Our kid don't need my money, he needs me, but I'll be damned if I ever go back to that gal. She robbed my spirit but she ain't going to get my soul."

He stops talking long enough to sing the refrain of a Willie Nelson song coming over the radio: "Don't boss him, don't cross him, he's wild in his sorrow, he's riding and hiding his pain." He's a cliché in a Chevy sedan instead of on a raging black stallion. He could be riding, though, his hand lying gently on the wheel, easing him in and out of traffic with the controlled motion of his wrist. His body is relaxed, his posture a reflection of a pint of vodka sipped through a night of desert highway and midnight cafes.

"Are you tired?" I ask.

"Nah, we change off driving and catch a few winks," Paul says. "I picked up Skeeter in the Mojave Desert and he was bright eyed and bushy tailed."

"Yeah," Skeeter laughs. "There was quite a show going on out there in the Mojave. All them jet bombers they have out at that Air Force base were doing all their practicing right over my head, diving and doing all kinds of crazy tricks and things."

"Those guys really are crazy, you know," Paul says. "I worked on jet planes when I was in the Navy, and I tell you, those pilots are crazy as loons. They can't wait to get up there and see how close they can get to each other without crashing, or see how high they can get before they start to pass out. I got out of the Navy pretty fast after I figured out how crazy those guys are, and how crazy this country is to let guys like that decide where the bombs are going to land."

"They sure were great, though," Skeeter says.

"Yeah, I guess so," Paul says. "If you got to be crazy it's best to be the ones dropping the bombs."

"Nowadays nobody has to drop the bombs, they just come out of missiles run by computers," I say. "Of course, someone has to push the button that sends the missiles so we spend twenty million dollars every four years to decide whether it should be a Republican or a Democrat."

"Yeah, but in Russia they don't even have a choice," says Skeeter. "It's always just that Brezhnev guy."

"I'll tell you," Paul says. "I've never understood why anyone would want to be president or premier or head honcho or whatever. I read in this psychology book once that said people like that are really insecure and unsure of themselves and they want to become presidents so they can throw their weight around and feel important."

"Sounds like as good an explanation as any they've ever offered," I say. "As for me, I'm just trying to find some hole to climb into that won't turn around and collapse on me."

Skeeter doesn't say anything for a while, then he turns to Paul, "Maybe there are a few men who still believe in doing what's right, and what's best for people."

"All very well and good, Skeeter," Paul says, "but who's to decide what's best for people? Mao Tse-Tung might decide it's best for the people that you not go to Sarasota and work for your uncle but accompany me to Oklahoma and raise corn for the masses. Richard Nixon might decide it's best for the people that you go to Miami and wiretap the Fontainebleau Hotel and spend the next ten years in jail. They're all crooks," Paul says. "You go find me one who's not, Skeeter, and I will personally kiss his ass."

Skeeter blushes, and we all sit back for a while, watching the scenery. Finally we crest the mesa above Albuquerque and we can see the city stretched out along the Rio Grande, winding through the valley. I try to imagine what it must be like seeing this sight for the first time, like Skeeter must be seeing it, with an unjaded view. Maybe it's still capable of startling the imagination.

"I haven't driven this highway in ten years," Paul says, sipping his vodka, "but I'll always remember coming up on Albuquerque like this. I've never stopped, though, just driven on through."

"Is that the Rio Grande?" Skeeter asks, pointing to the valley.

"Sure is," I say. "What's left of it."

"I've always wanted to cross the Rio Grande," he says. "But I thought I'd be in Mexico doing it, not Albuquerque."

Suddenly we all hear the sound of a siren. There, behind us, with flashing lights, is a state police car, bearing down.

"I was wondering where your cops was," Paul says, looking in the rearview mirror as he stashes the bottle under his seat. Then, quickly, the cop is around us, streaking by in the left hand lane, satisfied with a bonus scare in his pursuit of justice.

"That sonofabitch," Paul says, settling back in his seat. "I'm tired of feeling like a rabbit at a wolf's dinner party."

They let me off at the intersection of the freeways crisscrossing the state, stretching out in a hurry, anxious to get through these desert badlands. Paul wants to drive me to my door, but I won't let him. I pick up my dog and walk down the exit; the screams and fumes of the cars make her tremble in my arms. In another nine hours Paul and Skeeter will be in Oklahoma, and I will be lost in daily life. But we met for a minute out there, and I bet Hank Williams could have sung a good song about that, too.

Old Friends

My husband Andy drove up to Taos to get Willie. Willie was up there visiting another old friend who obviously didn't want him anymore. Now, according to Andy, these guys, Willie and Bob, had been friends since high school, soul mates, co-conspirators in the sixties' revolution of consciousness. They'd kept in touch for twenty years, until a shared history wasn't enough to connect a frustrated poet turned carpenter and a doctor turned cold and calculating. Andy was still a friend, though, and his loyalty had no limits, including our hospitality. I braced for two days of old-high-school-friends-turned-poetic-drug-takers-turned-cynical-world-travelers-steeped-in-male-comraderie-nostalgia.

First they had to dissect the doctor in Taos.

"He was my best friend, man" Willie, said, "and he couldn't respond to me at all. He couldn't take time out from his own preoccupations to look at me and feel for me as someone he loved and cared about."

"He's been really fucked up," Andy said. "I haven't seen him in over a year. The only time he ever calls is when Wanda threatens to leave him and he wants someone who will listen to him whine. I usually tell him he deserves any pain she's dishing out, but he doesn't want to hear that, obviously."

"Bob's an idiot not to get along with Wanda," Willie said. "She's got spunk—always has. Who else would have put up with his ravings all these years?"

"She's definitely his intellectual foil," Andy said. "Which is more than I can say about Crowley's new wife. She's very nice. And very beautiful. But she ain't in Crowley's ballpark." Crowley was another old high school friend, part of the same alumni conspiracy.

"Wanda is not Bob's intellectual foil," I said. "She is Bob's intellectual equal. Is your admiration for a woman defined by how well she puts up with a man? Wanda was a fool to have 'put up' with Bob all those years. Why should she have to 'put up' with anybody?"

"Hey, I love Wanda. She's a beautiful woman," Willie said. "She's a saint."

This guy is hopeless, I thought.

It was appropriate that Andy had just brought home some Richard Brautigan books from the library and I'd read this passage describing the character's girlfriend (or actually, Brautigan describing himself through the girlfriend describing her boyfriend): "She was never going to go out with another writer: no matter how charming, sensitive, inventive or fun they could be. They weren't worth it in the long run. They were emotionally too expensive and the upkeep was too complicated. They were like having a vacuum cleaner around that broke all the time and only Einstein could fix it."

Brautigan took the words right out of Willie's mouth. Two tequilas down the line and he was already sobbing about his wife who had finally divorced him and kicked him out of the house because he drank too much, couldn't earn a living, and keeping a failure around wasn't distracting her from her own failure anymore. "The upkeep was too complicated."

I'd met Willie's wife, years before, when we'd visited them in New York. I couldn't tell much from that visit, but according to Andy she had no interest in modern poetry at all. But she'd maintained an interest in Willie for ten years and an intense interest in their kids for the next ten.

The guy was really miserable, and I didn't want to be too hard on him—after all, he was Andy's friend—but I was really getting tired of the self-absorption. He was an interesting guy all right, but so are a lot of people.

"Why do you guys always assume your wives are going to be devoted to you because you're so interesting and they're so not?" I asked. "What I really don't understand is why you fall for them in the first place if you're looking for a soul mate, someone who is sympatica with your values and your dreams, someone you can discuss Jack Spicer with. Or are you always looking for a mother?"

Andy gave me a dirty look that said, lay off, this guy is hurting and you're just being defensive. Indulge him.

But I don't indulge anymore. That's what we're taught to do, you know. Indulge. Indulge a man's eccentricities, depressions, neurotic behavior because no matter how difficult they are to 'put up' with, things are always going to be more interesting with them around than without them. We'd die of boredom or suffocate from banality without them.

"Hey," Willie said, grabbing my hand and sobbing, "I want you to like me. I want to know you better. Don't you think I remember when you and

Andy came to stay with us? We showed the home movies of all of us—Andy, Crowley, Bob, Wanda, me and Sylvia. You're part of us. You're important to Andy and you're important to me."

"Oh my God," I said. "Don't patronize me. Please don't patronize me."

"Hey, you two, settle down," Andy said. "Willie, Marlys has been dragged through my past a million times and she's a little defensive."

"Andy tells me you're a great writer," Willie said.

"Oh my God," I said.

I drank another tequila, and Willie sobbed through the rest of the evening. In between bouts of crying he sat in our antique barber chair and read his poems to us.

"Isn't that a great one?" he said. "Doesn't that tear your guts out?"

"It's good, Willie," Andy said.

"Listen, Marlys, I want to know what you think of this one," he said, and read another poem. Then another. And another.

"I want you guys to respond!" Willie yelled at us. "This is my life's work, for God's sake."

"I'm listening, what do you want from me!" I yelled back. "Wow, that's great, hey, you're a great poet and you have every reason to be pissed off that nobody knows it."

"Some of them are very good," Andy said. "Just relax, Willie. We know you're a poet."

Soon papers of poems were littered all over the living room floor. Willie moved from the barber chair to the floor, to chain smoke cigarettes and shuffle through the papers.

"I want you to recite this one," he said to Cal, our four-year old son. "Come here."

Cal obediently went over to him, and Willie spoke each word of the poem and made Cal repeat each word after him. Luckily, it was a short poem.

"Did you like that poem, Cal?" Willie asked. "You're a poet, too, you know."

"I'm going to be a cowboy when I grow up," Cal said, and went back upstairs to play.

"He's a great kid," Willie said. "My kid Brian was like that when he was little. Never could tell him a thing, always had a mind of his own. Now he's a regular boy, plays football and baseball at school, locks himself in his room to play Twisted Sister records. He isn't doing that well in school, but at least he's normal. Ain't that something—I got two normal kids, interested in what other kids are interested in, who want to go to college and be an engineer and a lawyer. My middle class parents' genes skipped me and settled in my kids. They're perfect. They're just what they have to be."

"Yeah, they know they've got to get scholarships if they want to go to college. We sure as hell can't afford to send them," Andy said. "I hate to think about what it's going to be like when Cal is eighteen. I'll still be out there laying adobes for ten bucks an hour, struggling to pay the gas and electric conglomerates so we can have light and don't freeze to death. But, hey, any kid from New Mexico with anything on the ball can go to Harvard. Let Cal go to Harvard or Yale and support his parents in their senility."

These guys, talking about their kids winning scholarships and going to Harvard, were the dropout generation, for whom academia represented the bourgeois fulfillment of anal eggheads.

"Here's a picture of Marty," Willie said, showing us a pink-cheeked daughter of eighteen. "She'd be a beautiful kid if she lost fifteen pounds. But what the hell, she's got a National Merit Scholarship to Swarthmore and she's in love with some jerk in business administration. She's never smoked marijuana in her life and she doesn't even know who Jack Kerouac is. God, she's so naive," he sobbed.

I figured Sylvia had spent eighteen years making sure she came out that way. Here we were, Sylvia, Wanda, and I, newly divorced, soon-to-be-divorced, and as far as I could tell still solidly married to these three men whose lives were played out with desperate enthusiasm and unbearable angst. Sylvia, from some provincial Midwest town, went to New York and met this intellectual hippie named Willie who turned down a scholarship to Yale to run a live theater in the East Village. Sylvia knew how to act—intuitively, Willie said—and married the guy on stage after a showing of End Game. She stayed in the kitchen a lot when everyone came over at night to pop pills, smoke dope, and read poems. Willie always thought he was the director, even when the theater closed, the other poets got paid to read their poems, and two children came along demanding to be fed and clothed. Sylvia occasionally appeared in small, neighborhood productions, but mostly she stayed home and watched Willie realize he wasn't in control of anything.

"She never took any chances in her whole life except marrying me," Willie said.

Wanda, on the other hand, moved in with Bob and they read Charles Olsen together and she said, "Bob, I'm yours, teach me how to write and be psychedelic." And she followed him around the country to poetry readings and four years on the Navajo Reservation where he doctored up malnourished and alcoholic Indians in Tuba City. They had kids, too, and she mothered them and made a home for them and she continued reading Olsen and Ashbury and Whalen, too. But she was never able to write. Then their kids grew up and they moved to Taos so Bob could doctor overfed, tranquilized Anglos. Wanda discovered that she hated Olsen and all academic poets ("I shut the book if there's one reference to Greek mythology") and enrolled in a writing class taught by a midwestern woman poet who ran a bar in Taos.

And then there's me. And I supposedly know better, but here's this obviously bright, talented man confronting the tragedy of his life and I'm so worried about my own I can't even lend him some compassion. But then again, he'd never even lend me enough interest to know I warranted any.

Willie sobbed, I steamed, and Andy gave us both despairing looks until I couldn't stand it anymore and went upstairs to bed. Andy got Willie to bed soon afterwards, and I told him, "Get him out of here tomorrow, I'm not dealing with this for another twenty-four hours."

"I'll take him into town, buy him lunch, show him the sights," Andy said. "His plane leaves Tuesday morning, and I can't kick him out in the cold. I'm not going to be like Bob and desert him now when he needs me the most. Willie took me in years ago when I needed it, and I owe him at least that much."

"All right," I said. "I'm not a cold-hearted bitch, you know."

"I know," Andy said, cuddling close. "I don't know if I can take another day of this, either."

They went off together in the morning, I took Cal to nursery school, and then finished painting the upstairs. I didn't plan anything interesting for dinner, as Willie had cried through the previous evening's Chinese dumplings.

But when they came home they were sober and in a good mood and Willie sat on the floor and played with Cal while I baked a chicken. Andy told me they'd had some nice conversations, eaten carne adovada at Sadie's, and spent the afternoon seeing the Armand Hammer exhibit at the museum.

The tequila was gone, and we ate dinner in front of the TV watching Grand Hotel on the movie channel. Cal sat with us and we talked about who would win the NBA playoffs, cracked jokes, and told magic mushroom stories.

In the morning Cal and I hugged Willie and Andy put him on the plane back to New York, to a five-story walk-up in a semi-gentrified Avenue A apartment where he was going to live by himself for the first time in twenty years. Two weeks later he called Andy to tell him he owed him twenty dollars on the Celtic's win, and that's the last we ever heard from him. We both got depressed for a while after he left, and Andy told me he never wanted to talk to Bob again if he called. He never did, and although we're supposed to go up there for some party Wanda is giving, I think we're ready to forget them all as fast as we can and face our own limitations alone. Friends, like stories, are sometimes better old.

A State of Mind

They lived in an apartment only a few blocks from the bay. He would walk there in the morning, while the hired woman gave Hilda a bath. He always returned for lunch, though, to feed her himself. Sometimes, as he lifted the beef or herring or cottage cheese to her mouth too quickly, she would grab his hand and murmur, "Edward." Then he would sit there, disquieted by the sound of his name from the lips of this helpless woman, his wife.

After lunch, on the days when he didn't go out to play golf, they would watch T.V. She sat there, her chin resting in her hand, her legs crossed at the ankles, her eyes riveted to whatever it was she saw. He wasn't at all sure she saw anything, but he would talk to her about whatever was on. If it was a soap opera, he would laugh and ridicule the sentimentality and melodrama to hide his embarrassment at actually watching such a program. If it was a game show, he would try to make all the correct answers before the contestants did. "Jeopardy" was his favorite; he thought Hilda might be impressed by all the information he had amassed in his eighty-three years. It was patronizing, he knew, but it was less oppressive than silence.

Maria, the woman who came in during the day to help take care of Hilda, would cook them dinner before she left. She tried to teach them about enchiladas and chile rellenos, but Edward finally convinced her that he was too old to develop a tolerance for chile and onions. So she learned to cook briskets and lamb chops and an occasional filet of sole to remind them they lived near the sea.

They were friendly with a few people in their apartment building, particularly a man named Myron Silverstein. He had been a surgeon in Indianapolis until a stroke had crippled his hands. Now he was a surgeon of the mind, he said, and he had only one patient—God.

Sometimes Edward enjoyed his conversations with Myron; they both were thankful for the sagacity of their aging minds, and they argued for the sake of argument. But more and more often Myron was preoccupied with his psychoanalysis of God.

"He presents a classic case of schizophrenia, you know," Myron said to Edward.

"How is that?" Edward asked.

"Satan was His favorite angel, yet God was compelled to tempt Eve in the Garden of Eden and make Satan responsible for the ensuing sins of civilization. He created the world in six days and said it was good, but He was not content with what was good, or perhaps He could not define what was good without evil and He tempted mankind forever."

"I think you're being a little too literal, Myron," Edward said. "It's hard for me to discuss God as a schizophrenic when my conception of the gentleman precludes that definition."

"It makes perfect sense, though," Myron answered, "if all of us tortured souls are indeed created in God's image."

When Edward could find nothing more to say to his friend on the subject, they would talk of the places Edward had been on buying trips for a department store, and the interesting cases Myron encountered as a surgeon. Occasionally, after a martini or two, Edward would allow himself to talk to Myron about Hilda. It helped that his friend was a doctor; that way the conversation seemed more clinical than confessional.

"Senility is a very strange phenomenon, Myron," Edward said. "I understand the physical part of it—the deprivation of blood to the brain and the inhibition of both mental and physical activity—but I look at Hilda sometimes and I have to believe there's more to it, that she lives in another world, far removed from yours or mine, about which I can make no judgments. I feel so far away from her. The social workers at the hospital were being very presumptuous, I think, to tell me I would experience a father-child relationship with Hilda. She is gone from me completely."

"One never knows about these things," Myron said soothingly. "They say that some victims of strokes regress to the mental level of children, and that they are quite ignorant of what has happened to them. But there are those people, and perhaps Hilda is one of them, who seem even further removed from our consciousness, which leads one to believe that there is a busy, inner life which takes over when communication facilities break down. I have seen some patients who seem to have gone back to a time in their lives when things were very good for them, and they were happy. Consequently, they have no knowledge of the future, or of the fact that they are senile. It's the most desired circumstance, don't you think?"

"I suppose so," Edward said impatiently, "but that's not what happened to Hilda. I think it's far more complex than that. I think it's a world completely foreign to her experience, or yours or mine or anyone's. It's almost like she has awakened a consciousness that lay dormant, that could only be released when Hilda's perception of our world broke down and allowed her to recognize this inner life. She is now a different person, and I have very little meaning in her life."

"I don't think that the two need be mutually exclusive," Myron said gently. "Perhaps Hilda is very far away from us, but your love and support will always to vital to her well being. You should view her separateness as consolation, without denigrating your importance to her. Human contact is our only salvation."

So they would say good evening, and Edward would hold Hilda's hand and help her drink a martini. Later, she would fall asleep in her chair, and he would sit with her until his own eyes closed and his heart relented.

On Hilda's good days they were able to take short walks together down to the park by the bay. Maria would dress her in one of the fitted dresses that still hung in the back of the closet, reminders of her stylish days gone by. Hilda seemed to remember some of them, running her hands down the mauve, amber, and turquoise materials, feeling the expense. Edward covered Hilda with baggy, loosely knit sweaters to obscure the dresses, painful for him to remember.

It took almost an hour to walk the few blocks to the bay. Edward's legs longed to stretch and stride, to enjoy the spring still left in his step. Hilda used to complain that he walked so fast she felt like a Japanese wife, always two steps behind, keeping place. Now, he slowed his pace to match her stumbling gait, and they slowly made their way along the streets.

There was much to see. Elaborate flower gardens of brilliantly colored plants, fruit trees, and sculptured bushes filled the yards they passed. The air was redolent of a sickeningly sweet perfume, alien to Edward's nostrils, trained on the manmade New York City smells of car exhaust, street cleaners, and sidewalk pizza stands. He was still amazed at this voluptuous environment in which he now found himself, a foreign creature in this land of sunshine and plenty. At first he had found it almost vulgar, all this verdant green, blue sky, and moist air full of clear sunshine. Now, although he still looked at it with a wary eye, he appreciated the constant temperateness. Hilda never would have made it on walks through the snows of New York.

She, on the other hand, had seemed to acclimate readily. Maybe it was a function of senility, but she certainly seemed at home here in the sun. On one of their first visits to the beach she had removed her shoes and walked through the rolling waves, intently watching the blond-hair, brown-skin cloned surfers ride their boards. Edward sat on their towel and watched her watch, until she started to take off her clothes to join the surfers and rushed her back to their apartment.

At the bay they watched the sailboats glide back and forth across the harbor. They had sailed together, many years before, on summer vacations along the east coast, at expensive summer cottages on pristine beaches.

"It's not such a rich man's sport anymore, Hilda," he said, pointing to the proliferation of boats in the water. "See all those small boats called catamarans? All the young kids around here save their summer money and buy them like we used to buy bicycles. Remember that boat we used to borrow from Moishe, the twenty-five footer? We had some good times on that."

"Moishe is stingy," Hilda said.

"What do you mean, honey?" Edward said, surprised. "You always said Moishe was your favorite brother."

"Oh...," Hilda said, shaking her head. "Moishe and Ben pull my hair and make me cry. I don't like sailing. I have to throw up."

"You never told me Moishe and Ben were mean to you when you were a kid," Edward said. "I should have guessed your glowing picture of family life was a whitewash. You never were one for psychological examination of family relationships. It all comes out now, huh?"

"Where's Moishe?" Hilda asked. "Where's his boat?"

"Moishe is dead, darling," Edward said. "He died several years ago, remember?" Hilda had been grief stricken at the news of her brother's death, before she had become sick herself. Now that she has forgotten it, maybe she can keep a younger, happier version of him, Edward thought. Hilda had never been one to deal well with sickness or infirmity, mental or physical. She had always been too practical and robust, with little patience for anyone who wasn't. Thank God it didn't happen to me first, he thought.

"I don't miss the sailing either, you know," Edward said to her, "even if it's not bourgeois now. Maybe I should give up golf, too. It belongs in the same category," he laughed.

Hilda laughed with him, and he put his arm gently around her waist.

"We just have each other now, darling, don't we?" he said.

"I want to go home now," she said. "I don't want to go to Staten Island."

He didn't tell her she had the wrong ocean. It didn't matter anymore, really.

In the fall, following Hilda's second stroke, their children and grandchildren came to visit. In anticipation, Edward bought a quart of Jim Beam for his grandson, David, as he remembered that bourbon was his favorite drink. For his granddaughter, Loey, he bought lox for breakfast, remembering late night trips to the neighborhood deli in New York. For his son and daughter-in-law, he prayed for patience.

The day before his family came, he pulled out all the photo albums and sat with Hilda on the couch, thumbing though pictures of the past. He carefully selected the best likenesses of the family and showed them to Hilda. For this visit, he had to assume her participation.

"Remember this one, honey, taken of Arthur when he was elected to the city council in Rochester?"

"Oh, yes, I remember when he...," Hilda began, never finishing.

"You remember when he what, sweetheart?" Edward urged. He thought she recognized their son, but he wanted her to keep some special remembrance of him in her mind to connect the picture with the person who would be arriving the next day.

"Oh...," she murmured, wiping her forehead with her hand.

"That's all right, honey. Arthur will be here soon to help you remember."

He showed her next a picture of Helen, Arthur's wife, taken the previous year at the beach.

"Helen still has quite a figure, doesn't she?" Edward said. "Let's see, Helen is five years younger than Arthur, so that must make her fifty-five. She was always such a pretty woman. I wonder if Arthur is still aware of that."

He knew his son's marriage had been an uneven one, and although he loved them both he couldn't imagine living with either of them. They seemed to have modeled their marriage on the modern design where any semblance of compatibility was sacrificed to the principle that self-assertion was the truth and the light. He was always reminded of Arthur and Helen when he went to see the chimpanzees at the zoo. The female teased and harassed the male unmercifully, while the male beat his chest and displayed his pride in her courage.

The only recent picture he had of his granddaughter had been taken several years before when she had stopped to visit them on her way home to Colorado from a hiking trip to Alaska. In the photo she was frowning, her long nose pointing down over her rigid lips. She hated having her picture taken, and he knew why—the vibrancy of her flushed face, lightly freckled skin, and deep blue eyes became flat and dull on paper. He wanted to tell her it didn't matter, everyone saw only a person they knew and loved in the photo, not the caricature she saw. It was painful for him to see her vulnerability.

"Look how mad Loey is at me for taking her picture, Hilda," he said, showing her the photograph.

"Yes," Hilda laughed, looking down at Loey. "She's so beautiful...," she added, hesitantly rubbing her finger back and forth across the picture.

Edward stared silently at his wife. Before, Hilda had few kind words for their granddaughter. She had always told him that Loey disappointed her, moving off to some ski resort in Colorado when she should have finished college, become a professional, found a good man. Instead, she demeaned herself, teaching spoiled rich kids how to ski, living in a log cabin with dogs and cats and an occasional man. They never discussed the men. Edward couldn't help but laugh at his wife's aspirations for their granddaughter. His own such familial hopes had been more than adequately met by his son's success; now he could enjoy the vagaries of his grandchildren's lives with the abandonment of a generation's removal.

Hilda continued to rub the picture of Loey with her finger. Senility has sweetened you, my dear, he said silently to his wife.

He gently replaced the picture of Loey with one of David and his ex-wife Laura, seated in Arthur and Helen's backyard. They had been married only a few years, and Edward had met Laura twice. He remembered what a furor the marriage had caused. Laura was from a wealthy Rochester family that was unhappy its daughter had chosen David for a husband. He was Jewish, and he was a liberal—his politics were yet to complete their full swing to the left—but most pernicious was the fact that Arthur and Helen had joined the

Communist Party in the 1930s. Laura's father informed Laura of this fact and forbade the marriage. Laura informed David of this fact (the first he had ever heard of it) and he went delightedly to his parents for what he hoped would be their confirmation. When Helen and Arthur found out that Laura's father had hired a private investigator to investigate their "worthiness," they talked about suing for invasion of privacy, but when David and Laura married without her father's consent or attendance—and with considerable loss of inheritance—they were appeased by the loyalty of the new family member and the satisfaction of another family's loss. Edward took all of this in stride (Laura's father had neglected to probe any further than the parents), and, like David, was pleasantly surprised to hear of the Communist affiliation. He had tried to raise his son with a political and ethnic conscience, despite his own assimilated good luck. David only reached his political potential when the marriage was over; an avowed Marxist, he worked in the steel mills of Baltimore. Edward didn't envy his grandson's life, but he appreciated his fervor.

"David's coming, too, sweetheart," he said to Hilda.

"Is she coming, too?" Hilda asked, pointing to Laura.

"No, dear, she and David are no longer married. You remember, don't you, when they were divorced?"

Edward wondered what would have happened if divorce had been so commonplace when he and Hilda were young. Perhaps they, too, would have decided marriage wasn't worth it. But it was not so easy to decide that then. What would Hilda have done without a husband? She had no formal education, no skills, no business contacts to help her find a career. He looked at his wife, who had fallen asleep in her chair, and was startled to see that her delicacy and frailness, withered instead of fresh, were the same qualities which so many years ago attracted him. Her hair was still fine and henna colored (the beauty parlor kept it that way now; he took her there every month to send the red dye through any gray hair that appeared to shock him so), the sprinkle of freckles still visible across her nose. Would his wife have had a better life without him, without her role as the woman behind the man, raising his children, entertaining his friends, moving around the country to accommodate his business? Now she had only him, and for the last time he must prove himself worthy.

He leaned over and shook her by the shoulders.

"Hilda, I have to ask you something. Were you happy with me? Didn't we have a good life together, and you're not sorry for being my wife?"

With her eyes still closed she softly moaned, "Oh...."

The children came, and he watched them kiss Hilda, hold her hand, help feed her, and he saw how sorry they felt for him. One evening at dinner—Helen had cooked a wonderful roast—Hilda almost choked as a piece of meat became entangled with her false teeth. Arthur had to pull the meat out of her mouth. Everyone laughed, including Hilda, to cover their embarrassment. Edward put his head in his hands and cried; everyone immediately fell silent, except Hilda, who continued to laugh. He prayed that he, too, could understand the joke.

St. Lucy

Lucy, unlike Wendy, takes in both lost boys and girls. Most recently she's had a brother and sister from Rositas who were living in an abandoned adobe down on Lucero Creek, and a girl from Santa Fe whose mother was too busy channeling God's messages to the chosen to acknowledge any messages from her flesh and blood.

It's not like Lucy has the money or room to take them in, but that's usually the case, isn't it? Lucy and her husband Ole, a master builder, live in a high mountain valley in a four-room adobe house that lacks the amenities—running water, electricity, and gas for cooking. But Ole has made what's there extremely beautiful with his tools of trade. The ceiling is carefully coved around the vigas, the walls are troweled to a smooth finish, and the color is somewhere between rose and pink. It could be featured in *Better Homes and Gardens* if the magazine recognized beauty over chic. Into these four beautiful rooms rotate the assortment of kids Lucy takes in, eating her tofu manicotti and red chile burritos cooked on a wood stove next to a counter with buckets for sinks. Ole says a real sink is the next order of business—he feels sorry for Lucy washing the dishes outside in the snow.

Of course Lucy's own kids are another story. They both live down in Rositas with their father, Allen, because they don't like tofu and prefer hot showers to none at all. There they hang around with their friends, smoke cigarettes and act cool, while Lucy entices them home with promises of great hikes and apple pies. They periodically show up—often dragging their homeless and addicted friends with them for Lucy to take in—but they don't stay. So Lucy concentrates on her foster children and hopes for the best for her own.

The latest adoptee, Brad, is a fifteen-year-old kid from Rositas whose father is threatening to send him to military school in North Carolina to straighten him out.

"If Brad goes to North Carolina," Lucy tells Ole, "he'll either run away immediately or kill himself. So I'm keeping him here."

"What does his dad think about that?" Ole asks.

"He's too busy drinking to notice he's not there," Lucy says. "If I can just keep him up here long enough maybe his dad will forget he's alive."

"You're going to try to keep him all winter?" Ole asks. "What are we going to do for room if your girls decide to come home?"

"Oh, I think Emma's going to stay in school down in Rositas, she think's it's cool to be in high school now, and you know Rose can't stand to be up here more than two weeks at a time—booooooring, you know. So Brad can stay if he wants. I'll give him pep talks all the time, to show him if you wake up with a smile there's something to live for. But I'm sending Sally back—she drags around all day moping about her boyfriend, who beats her up and treats her like shit—and I can't compete with that, can I?"

"What about Dutch?"

"I think Dutch is going to be okay," Lucy says. "He's eighteen and almost on his own. I think he can make it. He signed on with the tree planting crew this fall, and he can chop wood for us for room and board. If I can only break Brad of his cigarette habit, maybe he can breathe this clean air and wash away the Satan shit in his head."

Despite the fact that none of these kids belong to Ole, he's tolerant of Lucy's brood. He goes to work while Lucy practices resurrection psychology, and on the weekends he climbs mountains and lives in his body while Lucy stays home and lives in her head.

One weekend Lucy persuades Ole that they should take Brad and Dutch on a hike up North Peak to breathe the air up there at 13,000 feet. While Dutch sucks it all in with delight, Brad's lungs and spirit are too filled with bile to breathe. A good-looking kid, with the sulk of James Dean, he is too full of himself to let go.

"Oh God, this is so beautiful," Lucy says, as they rest in the saddle before the final ascent.

"I'm not going any further," Brad says. He sits down on a rock in his trench coat, which he defiantly wears as a symbol of his alienation, and begins panting.

"Come on, man," Dutch says, "we're going to the top. We gotta see what the world looks like from the top, man." Dutch is dressed in shorts, sandals, and a t-shirt, even though the temperature at 13,000 feet, or almost 13,000 feet, makes this September day feel like November.

"I'm too tired," Brad says. "I can see fine from here."

"Brad, for once in your life you can be at the top, with just a little effort," Lucy says.

"That's a bunch of crap, Lucy," Brad says. "It's just the top of a mountain, a piece of rock. Don't give me your spiritual bullshit about climbing mountains to let your spirit be free. My spirit needs a cigarette."

"Why don't we stop here for a while and have some lunch before we make the final ascent," Ole suggests. "Maybe by then you'll have your second wind."

"I'm going on up," Dutch says, jumping across the boulder field that initiates the climb. "See you guys on top."

"Be careful," Lucy calls. "Look at Dutch, Brad, he's opening himself up to the experience, letting go of his personal baggage, making a break. His life at home is as lousy as yours—his mom and dad already kicked him out. But he holds on to what he knows is good. You've got to give yourself a chance. And I'm here to help you."

"Dutch gets on my nerves and so do you," Brad says. "What's for lunch?"

Lucy's made tempeh burger sandwiches, and after they eat Ole bounds off to join Dutch on top of the peak while Lucy sits by Brad.

"You can't go to North Carolina, you know," Lucy says. "It'll kill you."

"What am I supposed to do then?" Brad asks, puffing on a piece of grass. "My dad won't take me. If I show my face there it's off to the killing patrol."

"Ole and I want you to stay here with us," Lucy says. "You can stay in the girls' room and help Dutch cut firewood and Ole will teach you how to ski this winter."

"I hate winter," Brad says. "Maybe I'll let my dad put me on the bus to North Carolina and I'll just keep on going to Florida. They ain't got no winter in Florida."

"Florida is a horrible place," Lucy says. "That's where my parents and their friends go to sit around their condominiums and complain about their miserable lives. You have your whole life ahead of you, Brad. Let me help you find the person in there who can live that life with a chance for some love and happiness."

"I'm not interested in love," Brad says. "Satan is better than love."

Brad left and did get on the bus—Lucy didn't know if she was losing him to Satan or military school, or if there was any difference—but it didn't stop her from taking back Crystal, daughter of the Santa Fe channeler. It seems the mother's boyfriend decided that giving Crystal a black eye was God's message of submission that day. When Ole came home from work, Crystal was in the back bedroom, nursing her purple eye.

"Why don't we turn him in to the cops," Ole says. "He can't do that to children."

"The mom is the one we ought to turn in to the cops," Lucy says. "Did you know she makes thousands of dollars from people who come to use her as a medium to God or whatever power it is they think can save their miserable little lives. But we can't turn either of them in. It won't help Crystal. She has to leave on her own now and try to find her way with people like us, who care."

"How can she?" Ole asks. "She's never been loved."

"I know," Lucy cries. "I can only love her too late."

While Crystal is still in the back bedroom, Lucy's daughter Rose comes for a visit. Rose, who is thirteen, and Crystal, who is seventeen, smoke all the cigarettes Brad left in the house and take turns perming each other's hair. Lucy complains about all the noxious smells and sends them out to sleep in a tent in the yard.

"You can't just stop them smoking in the house, Lucy," Ole says. "You've got to stop them smoking, period."

"I don't stop children from doing anything," Lucy says. "I show them another way. They'll come back to me when they're old enough to be true to themselves, not to each other. Until then, I can only love them."

One day Crystal and Rose come home from a friend's house all giggly and weak.

"What's so funny?" Lucy asks.

"Nothing," they giggle, and collapse into their room.

"I think they're on something, Lucy," Ole says.

"Like what?" Lucy asks. "I think they're just silly."

"Like Ecstasy, or one of those other designer drugs," Ole says.

"How do you know?"

"Oh, I did Ecstasy a few times in my younger days," Ole says. "I remember feeling just like they're acting."

"I've never done anything like that," Lucy says. "What does it do to you? It must be an upper, judging from all the giggling in there."

"It's an amphetamine and psychedelic, but it's not that dangerous," Ole says. "It's not like coke or LSD. But they're still too young."

Lucy goes into the girls' room and bounces on the bed with them.

"I want some, too," she says.

"Some what?" they giggle.

"I want some Ecstasy," Lucy says.

"What are you talking about, Mom?" Rose says, rolling her eyes and jiggling her head.

"I know you're high," Lucy says, "and I want to be high with you."

"You won't like it, Lucy," Crystal says. "You're too cerebral already."

"Maybe it will cancel my own head out," Lucy says. "Who gave it to you? Do you have any more?"

Rose shakes her head no, but Crystal digs in her pocket and brings out a small white pill wrapped in cellophane.

"Oh good," Lucy says. "You don't have to snort it."

"Nope," Crystal giggles. "Just pop it in your mouth."

"Promise me I won't OD. I don't want to leave Ole alone."

"It's going to be fun," Crystal says and gives Lucy the pill. They all sit there until Lucy's head begins to break.

"Why am I seeing rabbits?" Lucy asks. "Why am I seeing American flags?" She bounces harder on the bed. "I don't like American flags. But the colors are pretty, aren't they, girls? Red, white, and blue. That's an interesting color scheme, except that it's on a flag that symbolizes everything that's wrong in this world, like patriotism. Do they still make you say the Pledge of Allegiance in school? I remember when the nuns used to make us put our hands over our hearts and recite the Pledge of Allegiance every morning before school started, standing out in the schoolyard, even if it was starting to rain or snow, which it always was in Cleveland. Cleveland is a terrible place. We're so lucky we live here in New Mexico. Cleveland is where old farts live, girls, did you know that? Old farts who haven't had an idea about anything in their whole lives except what's for dinner. Thank God I got out of there. Maybe that's what all these rabbits are—they represent all the old farts in Cleveland who go on multiplying and polluting the earth."

Crystal and Rose run for Ole. He has to spend the rest of the day with Lucy, listening to her talk about rabbits and flags. The girls disappear into their tent.

"I was right to choose this life, wasn't I?" she asks. "We must do everything in our power not to destroy the earth. I refuse to have a toilet, even if I had running water. I hate toilets. People just sit there and stink up the earth and don't even know it because they can just flush it away. They never see it or smell it or know that instead of flushing it away you can compost it and use it on your garden to grow vegetables you can eat to create good, clean shit instead of the dirty, foul shit of eating flesh. I refuse to pollute my body by eating flesh. I refuse to just flip a switch and pollute the air just to light up a room. Rooms are lit by human warmth and kindness. That's what I want to create—warmth and kindness, not darkness and death. What else is there to do?"

"Create revolutions," Ole says.

"I'm not angry enough," Lucy says. "I'm too full of love."

Ole goes out and makes the girls come in to cook dinner. By then Lucy is lying on her bed, exhausted. Ole holds her hand.

"They abandoned me," Lucy says. "I took that stupid drug to be with them, and they abandoned me."

"What did you expect?" Ole asks. "The last person a kid wants to see high is her parent."

"But I'm more than a parent to Rose," Lucy says. "I understand her. And I'm all Crystal has."

"It doesn't matter," Ole says. "I'm telling you, no one wants to see her parent out of control. Even if that's what they think they want. Did I ever tell you about the time my parents asked me to get them some grass? I must have been about twenty, living across town, and they said they were having a party with some of their friends and they all wanted to get high. So, stupid me, I brought some over and proceeded to get them all high as kites, and my mother completely freaked. It was the worst moment of my life. She got all paranoid and asked me how I could do this to her, and my dad had to take her upstairs and give her some valium."

"I didn't dump on Rose," Lucy says. "I wanted to take her with me."

"You can't," Ole says. "You're not going to the same place."

Lucy gets a postcard from Brad, who has indeed made it to Florida.

The card says, "Hi, St. Lucy. I'm here in Miami with lots of sun and beach and girls and beer. Don't tell dad. Wish you were here—Brad."

"He must be living on the street," Lucy says, showing the card to Ole.

"At least it's warm," Ole says.

"It may be warm," Lucy says, "but it's evil."

"Not like St. Lucy's, huh?" Ole says.

"It's the least I can be," Lucy says.

Giving Birth

You know right away it's a county hospital—I'm the only one in the room over twenty. The girl-woman across from me is nineteen, and the five-pound baby boy in the bassinet is her second child. They—the nurses in the nursery and on the postpartum floor—have a hard time keeping the baby awake long enough to take a bottle. I call this woman the Fox; as soon as she can walk she goes to the bathroom to put on her face.

The girl-woman next to me is twenty, and on her second baby as well. Her little baby boy weighs six pounds and has the longest hair I've ever seen on an infant. Thick and black, it stands straight out on end like a punk rocker's version of cool. The mother is very gregarious and nice, so I call her the Sweet One. At thirty-eight, I could be the grandmother of either baby.

I'm the only woman in the room who has a husband. Soon after each of us is admitted to postpartum, a woman from the vital statistics department comes around to collect data: our name, our husband's name, our baby's claim to legitimacy. My baby is the only baby who has a father's name on the birth certificate. There is a father around somewhere for the five pound baby across the room, though. I hear the Fox talking to him on the phone, asking when he is going to be in to visit.

"Hi, it's me. Yeah, I'm pretty tired. When you coming over? Oh, you have to go to your dad's to get some tools, huh? What's wrong? The carburetor? Why don't you call my mom and get her to bring you by after work. Okay, well, maybe I'll see you later. Oh, the baby's fine, except I can't get him to wake up to take a bottle."

The Sweet One is listening, too.

"Was that your husband?" she asks.

"He's my boyfriend," the Fox answers. "His car broke down so he has to go fix it. I'm still married to my little girl's father, but he's in the State Pen and I don't see him no more."

"What did he do?" the Sweet One asks.

"He killed another guy in a fight," the Fox answers.

"Oh, that's too bad," the Sweet One says. "He'll probably be in for a long time, huh?"

"The longer the better," the Fox laughs. "Where's your little boy's father?"

"I don't know," the Sweet One says. "My little girl and I live with my folks."

"How old is your little girl?"

"She's three," the Sweet One says.

"Oh, that's the same age mine is. You know, I used to want a lot of kids, at least five or six, but I'm going to stop having babies after this one, it hurts too much."

"Did your baby come out the right way?" the Sweet One asks. "I had to have a caesarean this time, my baby was breach. My little girl came out real easy, so this one was much worse."

"I was in labor for fifteen hours with my little boy," the Fox says. "I thought I was going to die."

I was in labor for fifteen hours, too, and while I knew I wasn't going to die, I wanted to. After fifteen hours and only three centimeters dilation, I was mad at everyone, and afraid. I yelled at my husband when he tried to make me breathe, and I cursed my doctor when she told me that every contraction made me closer to delivery.

What we were close to, though, was the emergency mode. The baby's heart rate drops—maybe the cord is wrapped around its neck—and suddenly an oxygen mask is slapped on your face, they're running you down the hall, someone sticks a tube up your urethra, and then they say, count to four and you'll be gone. My husband is there, holding my hand, and I silently say goodbye, just in case.

Then, forty-five minutes later I wake up in a small, white room and they bring me my son. He's already been suctioned and poked and prodded and cleaned of my vernix and fluids and I've missed it all, my body a piece of meat on the table. My husband tells me later that they had a hard time getting him out of the incision, his head was so big. Two people pulled and two people pushed and he finally popped out. Now he's here, crying and mourning this shocking, painful taste of life outside the womb, and he attaches to my breast, desperate for comfort.

My baby doesn't sleep for two days while the Fox's baby won't wake up. A nurse comes in to take her baby for his bath or some test or just out of plain possessiveness and asks, "Haven't you made him wake up yet? You have to tickle him and poke him until he wakes up. He has to eat."

I won't let them take my baby, although he can't sleep and I can't sleep and can hardly move. I nurse him continuously until my nipples are red and cracked and swollen, but it's the least I can do. The Fox sleeps most of the day while her baby stays in the nursery. The Sweet One visits with her three year old and her parents—small, stocky people who don't say much—and chats with anyone who comes by.

Great assortments of people come by. Every morning, the residents come, earnest young men armed with charts and stock phrases. They ask questions but provide no answers.

"What kind of birth control will you be using?"

"Will you be breast feeding or feeding with formula?"

"Do you want your baby circumcised?"

The Sweet One calls someone on the phone and asks, "They want to know if I want the baby circumcised? What should I do?"

No, I silently scream. There's no reason to mutilate your beautiful baby. Why don't the doctors tell her this? Why does the hospital circumcise as a matter of course? But the Sweet One's advisor tells her differently and off they go to a place I don't want to think about.

After the residents are gone the picture lady comes in. Dressed in clingy rayon and stiletto heels she wants to dress our babies up in miniature tuxedos or Santa Claus suits and take their pictures for thirty dollars. I tell her I'm a photographer myself, but the Fox and the Sweet One pour over the sample pictures she shows them of brown babies, yellow babies, black babies, white babies, all dressed to inhabit some weird adult persona. She explains they can pay the pictures off at five dollars a month. They both order the full package.

The Medicaid people are next. They don't bother with me. Too poor for insurance and too rich for welfare, I'll be signing my own checks for the next ten years to pay off my six thousand dollar baby. The other women will sign no checks, but their costs are enormous: the loss of any personal privacy, the subjugation to a system that defines their worthiness by the size of a welfare allotment that keeps them barely alive. Perhaps these children are their only consolation. Perhaps there is no consolation.

The Fox and the Sweet One reveal the intimate details of their lives to an anonymous government employee who barely makes more than she would if she quit her job and joined them on welfare. To make herself feel better about that she revels in the hardship of their lives.

"How many rooms are there in your house?"

"Four rooms."

"Do you have cooking facilities?"

"You mean a stove? Yeah, we got a gas stove."

"It says here you're not married."

"I live with my boyfriend."

"Do you heat your house with gas, too?"

"No, there's a gas heater in the living room, but we can't afford to run it so we use a wood stove."

"How many cars do you have?"

"My boyfriend has a car."

"Is it worth less than $3,000?"

"It's not worth anything when it don't run, which is most of the time."

"Does your boyfriend contribute to the support of your children?"

"No, he only contributes to the support of his habit."

Nothing embarrasses them anymore. The Fox tells the Sweet One her boyfriend is in a methadone program. The Sweet One tells the Fox how much she would like her own house because her father is too mean to her little girl, he expects too much. I can't tell them anything, and lie with my curtain closed just enough to remove myself from their atmosphere of confidentiality, but not appear too unfriendly. After my walks, I stop by their beds to look at their babies and admire them. I offer no advice, and no information about my husband, my home, my prognosis so much better than theirs. That is my judgment, and that is why I'm not a part of their conversation.

The Fox is released first. Her mother and boyfriend come to help her pack, and they dress the baby in a blue velour sweat suit. He sleeps through it all. I wonder what his life will be like in that four-room house. I wonder if his young mother will love him enough through all the sleepless nights and frustrating days so he may grow into his humanness with a little grace.

I go next, into the bosom of my family, where babies are born of great deliberation, care, and privilege. Will their lives be better for it, for the self-consciousness of their conception and the drama of their birth? The Sweet One eagerly accepts the flowers we can't fit into the car, and puts them next to her bed.

Just before we leave, a resident comes in, checks her chart, and says, "Have you had a bowel movement yet?"

"No," she answers.

"Do you have any discomfort in your intestinal tract?"

"No," she says.

"Well, you will if you don't get out of bed more and start walking," he says. "And we're not going to release you until your system is working properly."

"But it hurts so much to get out of bed," she says.

"Everyone has to walk," he says.

They wheel me out of the hospital, babe in arms. The sky is still blue, the wind blows cold across my face, and I'm going home with this fragile, helpless child in my arms. There will be no nurses, doctors, statisticians, or welfare workers to monitor my vital signs and my baby's precious existence. The Fox and the Sweet One will be on their own, too. Good luck to us all, and to our children, who will need it.

Great Things

He hit the Volkswagen on the Dome Valley road going thirty miles an hour over the potholes and limestone rocks spearing the air. The front end of the little car crunched, and he came out swinging, furious that his progress up the hill had been blocked. The woman in the Volkswagen flew out of the car and ran off into the piñon-juniper hills. The man, her husband, swore silently and prepared to protect his life.

"Do you want to fight?" the crasher said, the only thing he could think of to say that befit the occasion. He supposed the man in the Volkswagen would want to battle for his car.

"Oh, Jesus, I'm not asking for a fight, buddy, but you sure as hell screwed things up here," the man in the Volkswagen said bravely, looking at the crasher's devilish curls, golden earring, and tattooed cheek. He looked around for his wife and sighed.

"You shoulda got out of the way, man," the crasher said, dropping his fists and leaning over to inspect the damage. "I really did a job, didn't I?" suddenly grinning. "But I got to go fast over this road, man, so my kidneys don't have time to realize what's happening and vacate the premises. Besides, I'm drunk as a skunk. I'll tell you what. You come on down to the old convent in Alamita and ask for Stix and I'll fix you up good as new. I know where I can find a great little fender off a junked bug down by the river, and I'll just put it right on her and you'll never know the difference, except that it's blue and your little car here is green. But don't come on Sundays—I don't do no work on Sundays."

He turned around and climbed back into his truck. Turning on the engine he sat there, humped over the steering wheel, waiting. There was nothing the Volkswagen man could do but climb back into his banged up bug and move out of the way. The crasher roared by, waving out the window, and disappeared up the road. The wife appeared out of the bushes a few minutes later, sat down on the sagging bumper, and cried.

A woman came to the door when the Volkswagen man and his crushed car appeared at the convent several days later. He'd been to a party there once and met the once famous SDS agitator who owned the former nunnery. The man told him he had bought it to start a holistic health center, but everyone wanted holistic health for free, so he rented it out to the perpetual poverty line members of the community instead. He figured that was the next best thing.

"Is Stix here?" the Volkswagen man tentatively asked the woman in the doorway.

"Hi. He's around back working on his car." She smiled at him and came out of the building to show him the way. Her hips swayed nicely, but he was more interested in her belly button, pierced through with a turquoise earring.

They came around a corner and he saw a pair of legs sticking out from under a half black, half yellow jeep.

"Hey, someone, hand me a hammer," the legs said.

The Volkswagen man squatted down and offered the hammer to a blackened hand shoved out from beneath the car. The invisible hand pounded for a few minutes, and then Stix's head appeared, carrying a heavy load of New Mexican grit.

"Hey there, man, I was wondering if you'd show up."

"I wasn't quite sure you remembered what you said the other day," the Volkswagen man said shyly. "Alcohol tends to make promises fade away sometimes."

"I always keep my promises, man," Stix said in a steady voice. The Volkswagen man prepared to run. Then, in a completely friendly manner, Stix added, "Yeah, I remember one time going to a party in Montrosa, you know, with all them uranium miners they got there, and the next thing I knew I woke up in the solar dome up in Dome Valley. That's a hundred miles I ain't accounted for yet, but I guess a hundred miles ain't bad for thirty-five years of living. Not that I'm accountable for any of it, actually. If I was, someone would have done me in years ago—and here I am still kicking."

"I live up in the solar dome now, you know," the Volkswagen man said. "It's quite a place to wake up in, isn't it?"

"Man you ain't kidding. The only reason I woke up as soon as I did was that it started raining and the water came pouring in on my head. It was like waking up in a cowshed, with leaks all over the place, only I was there instead of a cow, and cows don't wake up with hangovers from drinking whiskey. That's one crazy house up there. You fixed up any of those leaks?"

"I tried to, but every time you fix one a new storm comes along and those damned car tops contract and break another seal. So I spread my plants around all over the floor and sleep in my tent."

The dome to which they were referring sat up on a hill in what everyone called Dome Valley, a concept of the sixties in the middle of the New Mexico desert. Built by an aspiring solar architect and communal theorist, the red, blue, green, yellow, and black dome was comprised of junked car tops whose sensitivity to the sun and rain rendered them useless. The communal effort had pretty much been rendered useless, too, but the dome, and several duplicates, remained. They were rather beautiful, standing together to form an extravagant contrast to the uniformly blue sky and red desert hills of the valley. Families lived in them now, raising kids in the aura of the one-time commune, if not the fact.

"So let's go get that fender, man. Hop in." Stix leaped into the front seat of his yellow and black jeep and turned on the engine. A roar invaded the convent, accompanied by shots of carburetion trying to equalize oxygen and gas. The Volkswagen man climbed up to ride shotgun, and they tore out of the convent onto the streets of Alamita, joining the parade of cruising Chevy's and Fords lowriding the hours away.

"Say, man, what's your name?" Stix yelled above the muffler roar.

"Andy. Andy Greenberg," the Volkswagen man yelled back.

"Was that your wife I scared off into the hills, Andy Greenberg?"

"Yes, that was my wife. My soon not to be wife, though."

"I'll tell you something, Andy. Never marry them. Live with them and love them and have kids with them and fight with them but never marry them. It's every man for himself and every woman for herself and all marriage does is try to con you into believing it ain't so. But it is."

They roared down to the Rio Grande and turned south along the irrigation ditch, sinking into its sandy banks. Sand invaded their nostrils and mouths, eyes and hair, until Andy began to resemble Stix. He started to think like him, too. I'm going to see Joan tomorrow and tell her to go to Legal Aid and start the divorce proceedings, he thought. This is a new land, and I'm going to be a new man in my aesthetic Dome Valley life. I will never again attempt to fix a leak.

They drove along the river bosque, the salt cedars brushing against the black paint job, polishing its dull color with feathered branches. On the other side of the river the desert rose to red mesa tops, their gullied sides providing access to Indian ponies running from the reservations. The ponies liked to mingle with the local horses, inverting the invasion of 300 years before when the Spanish had conquered New Mexico. Andy and Stix were part of the newest invasion—transplanted Anglos in yellow and black jeeps gleaning new life from the desert. Its eroding sands were somehow able to manage all three, Anglo, Spanish, and Indian in an Americanized version of third world culture.

Stix suddenly swerved the jeep onto an access road heading away from the river towards the farmhouses at the edge of town. Not far up the road Andy saw the blue Volkswagen standing upside down against a cottonwood tree.

"Some dude thought the tree was gonna move, looks like," Stix laughed, slamming the jeep to a stop a foot away from the smashed car. He jumped out and began pounding furiously at the bug's fender.

Andy cautiously looked around for an irate owner to come storming out of the bushes to protect his property, crumpled as it was. He always felt a little intimidated in Alamita, a stranger in an even stranger land of lowriders and beautiful black-eyed women who swung down the streets in high-heeled boots and obviously lost innocence. He never spent much time there, except to buy his beer and do his laundry. At the laundromat he often fantasized about meeting one of the Indian girls who came there from the surrounding pueblos, and taking her home with him to his dome. But the ones he wanted were always with their mothers. Besides, half the fantasy was sustained by the myth of their alienage, by the barriers of separateness that would never be broken. So he watched.

"Hey, Stix, what if this VW belongs to someone in one of those houses over there?" Andy asked, after Stix had the fender halfway off.

"Hey, man, it's cool, don't worry. I bet the dude who smashed it is sitting over there right now laughing to himself at us dumb hippies always trying to get something for nothing. He's probably riding around in a Ford Mustang right now, thanking his lucky stars he finally got this pipsqueak of a car off his hands."

With one tremendous jerk he pulled off the fender and threw it into the back on the jeep."

"Let's do it, man," Stix yelled, as they roared off down the ditch bank back to Alamita.

Stix was still installing the new fender when Andy decided to hitchhike back up the highway to Dome Valley, promising to return later that evening to celebrate the Volkswagen's resurrection with a shared bottle of tequila. He got a ride as far as the little village of Rositas, where the bruising road up to Dome Valley began. Rositas had been there for hundreds of years, one of the original Spanish land grant settlements, two connecting dirt roads of adobes and trailers belonging to the grandparents, children, nieces, nephews, and cousins of a handful of Hispano families. When the Anglos began arriving in the sixties, they grabbed up all the leftover land and created Ranchos de Rosita and Dome Valley. The latter was funky enough to fit the local decor, and the inhabitants considered themselves real New Mexicans, with enough trashed cars and arroyo junk heaps to prove it.

Andy walked through the village and headed up the Dome Valley road into the hills of piñon and juniper vegetation surrounding this spot of civilization. He remembered when it had been only a spot on the map to him, a possible solution to a dissolving marriage and a sedentary life in the snow of New England. He had come to visit an old friend who told him he had discovered the American Tibet. When Andy had seen Dome Valley, he knew it was going to be more than a visit. It was like science fiction, fantastical and surreal, full of colored domes and homemade adobes set against the sparse New Mexican vegetation and the blue, cloudless days of burning sunshine. It appealed to his imagination, and to his listlessness. The solar dome had been empty; he moved in in July.

He had written Joan about what he saw and felt; she had shown up in August. She didn't like sleeping in a tent, and the marriage still seemed to be dissolving despite the assuaging landscape, so she moved into a house in Rositas. She had been his high school sweetheart, one of the biggest catches in school, with a reputation to frighten away most suitors. But Andy had pursued her diligently and had won her heart with his stamina. He always suspected part of his appeal had been an unspoken promise to elevate her along with him as he aspired to "great things." She might have the looks and the guts and the reputation, but everyone assured Andy that he was the one who would achieve great things. It had been easy enough to believe them, and easy enough to believe in great things.

So they lived through the sixties together, and they shared the intense living those years demanded. When it was time to do something else, though, to graduate from their twenty years' adolescence, they were left staring at each other's failures. Andy was approaching thirty, the time when child prodigies had procured their fame or become alcoholics. He had to do something, so he went on an extended vacation two thousand miles away. There he found Dome Valley, and he wanted it to be his, not his and Joan's. He wanted a separate life, to aspire again in new modes. Dome Valley almost made one believe again that life could be profound. But there was still Joan, and they shared a history.

In the solar dome he cooked himself an omelet for dinner, with eggs from his neighbor's chickens. The sun set, and illuminated by the full moon, his dome shadowed the sky like a mosque. He'd already had a few religious experiences there, or at least he had interpreted them as such. That was easy to do, too.

After dinner he finished off his bottle of tequila, gathered up enough money for a new one in Alamita, and descended to Rositas. Joan was there, baby-sitting the neighbor's kids for gas and spending money.

"That crazy guy who hit us really did fix the VW," he said. "I'm supposed to go down and celebrate with a bottle of tequila. Why don't you come along? I'm sure there will be a party before long." He wanted to make amends for her tears.

"I can't," she said. "I have to take care of the kids."

"We can bring them with us," he said. "I want you to come with me."

She laughed and said, "Why do you suddenly want me to come with you? You've been complaining ever since I got here that I'm invading your territory, limiting your life."

"Oh, come on, let's go have a good time without arguing and dragging along our excess baggage," he said.

"I can't."

"Why?"

"Because my friend Jimmy is coming over to keep me company."

"Your revenge is without mercy," he said.

"I figured you'd see it that way," she said.

He left and caught a ride down the road with Tara, who lived with her goats and chickens and fatherless children in a crumbling adobe in the village. He asked her to the party. They found Stix sitting on Andy's Volkswagen, drinking a beer.

"She looks pretty good, don't she?" he said, patting the VW. "I'd have painted it for you, too, but I didn't know what color you wanted."

Andy looked at the black and yellow jeep and said, "That's okay, Stix. Blue and green are just fine."

The rest of the convent tenants drifted over, and the drinking began. A couple of guitars and a fiddle appeared, and Andy danced with Tara until his jellied legs dropped him to the warm, caliche, New Mexico ground. They sat up against the trunk of a cottonwood and attempted to flirt.

"You're really quite a woman, you know, raising all those kids and animals without someone to help you," he said, offering her a drink out of a bottle of bourbon he had found somewhere. He recognized the undercurrent of despair with the mixture of liquors.

"Oh yeah," Tara said, sighing. "I'm quite a woman all right. I'm so much a woman, and my two kids are so much two kids that any man would be a fool to want to help." She leaned over and kissed him on the cheek. "Don't let us fool you, honey, before your New Mexico worship wears off. It may be beautiful and inspiring and spiritually enlightening, but it's still life."

He gazed at her with drunken solicitude. "I still think you're wonderful."

The last thing he remembered was her fondling him, in the dark, under the cottonwood. He awoke with the sun, on a mattress. Across the room he saw Stix, lying on a bed with his arms around the turquoise studded woman. He checked his own bed to see if maybe a woman lay with him, too, but it was empty. As his head rolled around the room in a hangover haze, he saw Stix turn over and wink at him.

"Hey, man, it's okay. The sun decided to come up after all." Stix reached up and pushed open the door, letting in the sunbeams sprinkling across their faces. They crinkled Andy's eyes and tickled his nose, until he sat up and said to Stix.

"How many hours was I unaccountable for?" Then he lay back down and added, "You're wrong, Stix, it's all karma, and it'll haunt you for the rest of your life." The sun continued to shine and he sighed, "At least I can be a failure in crystal clear conditions." He rolled over and went back to sleep.

Riding the Bus

Laurel finally quit driving when she couldn't get in the driveway without jumping the curb and smashing the iris in the parkway. She left the car there one day, on top of the iris, and waited until her neighbor came by and moved it into the garage. All her children had been coveting it for years, with its classic slant-six engine, so she told them whoever they decided was in the most desperate need of a car could have it. So far, it was still in the garage.

She started riding the bus to the grocery store, the doctor's office, and to classes out at the University. Her friends who still drove came by and picked her up to go to circle suppers at the houses of fellow church members, or out to lunch at new restaurants in town. She hated to ask anyone for favors, so if she wanted something at the hardware store, or bedding plants for her garden, she waited until someone offered.

One day, waiting for the Wasatch bus that took her to the grocery store, she inadvertently got on the Fillmore bus and ended up at the new shopping mall at the north end of town. Not one to waste an opportunity, she wandered around the mall looking at all the stores, and spent the afternoon sampling the food from each of the booths that surrounded the second floor waterfall.

When she got home, tired but satisfied, she pulled out her bus schedule and saw how many other bus routes there were that she had never followed. She decided that, starting the next day, she would ride every bus in town, just to see where it went. She called up her friend Lucy to tell her about her plan.

"Why would you want to do that?" Lucy asked. "I'll be happy to drive you anywhere you need to go."

"No, no, Lucy. I want to ride the buses," Laurel said. "I think it will be fun. I never even went all these places when I could drive. I want to see what's happening to this city while I can still distinguish a bank from a church."

"How are your eyes, dear?" Lucy asked.

"The same," Laurel sighed. "No better, nor worse. I'll know when I've changed categories from 'visually impaired' to blind when I can't find my spectacles that keep me 'visually impaired'."

"Now Laurel," Lucy said. "Would you like to go to lunch tomorrow?"

"No, thanks, Lucy, I'm going to ride the Manitou bus tomorrow. I haven't been out there in ages. I'll watch for any new restaurant we might want to try."

The next day she put on her most comfortable summer pantsuit and caught the Weber Street bus down to Pikes Peak Avenue, where she could transfer to the Manitou line. There were only a few people on the Weber bus, as usual, mostly older people, and a young mother with her two children. Everyone else was out jogging, riding bicycles, or driving expensive foreign cars. This town is getting too rich for me, she thought, taking a seat next to the door. My house is the only one left on the block not painted some exotic color scheme of blue and red and purple, the favorite colors of the Victorian renovators. Even the house next door, with its four small apartments filled with transient tenants (except for the permanent black man upstairs who her children told her was called a Rastafarian, with his hair in dreadlocks down to his waist), had succumbed to a brown-orange-cream color scheme. The landlord has to protect his investment, she guessed. At least the Valiant is locked up in the garage now, where no one can see its peeling paint and retread tires.

At the Pikes Peak terminal she got off and found the Manitou bus already waiting beside the curb, spewing diesel fumes into the air. She took a seat facing center, so she could look straight ahead out a window, avoiding a possible sore neck. The bus sat there for ten more minutes while passengers straggled aboard—mostly tourists headed for the attractions of Manitou, geared especially to them. Just as the driver shifted gears and started to close the doors, another passenger pushed up the stairs.

"Always trying to close the doors in my face," the passenger muttered, plopping down in the seat across from Laurel. "They never do that to the young chippies in tight skirts and vampire make-up," she added, to no one in particular.

Laurel tried not to stare, but she couldn't help it. The woman across from her had on the most bizarre set of clothing she'd ever seen on a hot July day. She was wearing a wool cardigan sweater under a vest, a wool hat pulled down over her ears, black wool stockings under a plaid kilt skirt, and rubber boots. She carried a plastic shopping bag and a camouflage poncho over her arm. Colorado Springs' own brand of bag lady, Laurel thought.

She tried looking over the woman's head, out the window, as the bus traveled down Colorado Avenue. But all she saw was the crunched up face under a wool hat, and kept thinking of the sweat that must be trickling down the woman's scalp, into her ears.

"That's the only Goodwill in town that's worth beans," the woman said, pointing out the window. "Everything's under a dollar. The others ain't for the poor anymore, they're for the young chippies trying to dress like their mothers did in the fifties and willing to spend the money to do it. I do all my buying right here where they've got decent clothes at a decent price."

Laurel looked at the woman and realized this information was addressed to her.

"I know, the Goodwills do seem to charge too much these days," she answered. "Aren't you hot in those wool clothes?" She hadn't meant to say it, but she couldn't help herself. The thought of how the woman must be sweating upset her terribly.

The bag lady ignored her questions. "Nothing cheap these days, huh? You been out to that new Bag 'N' Save out on the Academy bus line? They take a couple of cents off the price and make you wander around all day trying to find where the hell everything is in that goddamn warehouse. And then you have to stand in line for an hour at the checkout stand when I already got all my stuff in my bag anyway. They treat the poor like dirt and expect us to be grateful." She pulled herself to her feet and yelled at the bus driver, "Hey, mister, this is my stop."

The bus driver leaned heavily on the brakes and pulled over to the curb. The bag lady lost her balance and Laurel grabbed hold of her to keep her from falling.

"Sonofabitch," the bag lady said. She collected herself and climbed down the stairs to the street, then up onto the curb. She turned and yelled at the bus driver, "If I was one of those young chippies you would have made sure the bus was right up against the curb."

The bus driver slammed shut the doors and pulled away. Laurel heard him mutter under his breath, "Old hag."

She was embarrassed. Mainly she was embarrassed for her fellow creatures, that they could be so ugly to each other, but she was also embarrassed that apparently the bag lady spent a lot of time riding the bus lines, too. Maybe this wasn't such a good idea. Laurel wasn't prepared for an affinity with someone so obviously crazy. I'll finish this ride today and see how I feel tomorrow, she thought.

She concentrated on the scenery now, as the bus passed through the newly renovated area known as Colorado City. The sidewalks had been laid with red bricks, old-fashioned lampposts lined the street, and specialty stores had replaced the bars, fleabag hotels, and pawnshops. When Laurel had first moved to Colorado Springs, thirty years before, Colorado City was the place where the dispossessed found cheap comfort and anonymity among their own kind. It was like Larimer Street in Denver, where the boutiques had changed the nature of the ghetto from squalor to chic. I wonder where all the poor people go now, Laurel thought. Somewhere she had read that the poor people in New York City, pushed out of their "gentrified" homes on the lower east side, were now living under Grand Central Station.

Manitou was the same, though. Even thirty years ago it catered to the tourists, with its mineral water bathhouse, penny arcade, motels, gift shops, Indian jewelry stores. Nestled at the foot of the mountains, it was the stepping off point for all excursions into the Rocky Mountains.

Laurel leaned forward and asked the bus driver, "How far does the bus go?"

"We turn around up at the end of Manitou Boulevard, just before the pass."

"Would you let me off at the next stop, please," she asked.

"Sure, lady."

She got off in front of Patsy's Popcorn Stand, which had always been there. Buying a box of caramel popcorn, she wandered around the Penny Arcade. The games and pinball machine were still there, and so was the bathhouse, but it had been renovated to keep up with the times. Individual hot tubs had replaced the former pool, and a sign on the door advertised the Deprivation Room, where one could lie naked in a tub of body temperature water in complete darkness to experience an absolute lack of stimuli. A few new shops had moved into the bathhouse, too—an import store, a stained glass studio, and a macramé shop. Laurel didn't bother going into any of them. She didn't need deprivation, fancy clothes, or more junk to clutter her house; these days she spent her money with immediate gratification in mind.

Well, I guess I've seen all I want to see, she thought, finishing her popcorn. Patsy's was worth the trip. She crossed the street to wait for the return bus. The same driver stopped the bus two feet away from the curb to let her on. She expected a pleasant "hello" or a "leaving so soon?" but he didn't seem to remember who she was.

"Sonofabitch," she muttered under her breath.

The next day she decided she'd try it again. This time she chose a bus heading east, out towards all the new developments stretching the city's boundary in typical urban sprawl. This will be a lesson in modern trends, she thought. No room today for nostalgic images and sentiment. Maybe I'll spot some good restaurants, though. They're all moving out east where the new money is.

She transferred to the Murray bus on Platte. There, in the same seat, sat the bag lady. Laurel started to turn around and get off. Don't be silly, she told herself. You can't let someone like this ruin your day. I have a purpose, a goal, a mission to see. She sat in her same seat, too.

"So it's you again," the bag lady said. "You going to the Goodwill on Platte?"

"No, not today," Laurel said. "Are you?"

"No, I told you, I don't go to no Goodwill's except the one on Colorado. I'm riding out to Memorial Gardens. I want to see my grave."

"How can you have a grave if you're still alive?" Laurel asked.

"Where I'm gonna have a grave when I croak, lady," she said. "You got a grave out there?"

"No," said Laurel. "I don't spend my time worrying about death. I have better things to do."

The bag lady looked her over carefully. "You're as close to the grave as I am, honey, so you better start doing some worrying about it or you'll end up in some wooden box in a pauper's grave. I'm making sure I'm gonna be buried in a lined casket out at Memorial Gardens where it's nice and green and shady."

"Where do you live now, if you don't mind my asking," Laurel said.

"I don't mind you asking if you don't mind me telling you you're nosy. Where do you think I live on a fixed income from lousy social security? Like all the rest of 'em I live in a dumpy apartment at the Acacia Hotel where they freeze you out in the summer and burn you up in the winter."

"Is that why you wear all that wool clothing?" Laurel asked, figuring this time she'd get an answer.

"What I wear is my business," the bag lady said.

Laurel turned her head to look out the window. Why am I trying to have a rational conversation with this woman? The bus was out by Academy Boulevard now, where rows of apartment complexes were interspersed with small shopping centers, enabling one to go directly from car to apartment to shopping center to swimming pool and Jacuzzi without ever leaving asphalt.

"Memorial Gardens is the next stop," the bag lady said.

"I couldn't care less," Laurel said, in the severest tone she could muster.

"Suit yourself, lady. Hey, mister, this is my stop."

When the bus stopped, Laurel followed her off.

"Decided to tag along, huh?" the bag lady said. "If you like mine you can go right into the office and order one for yourself."

Laurel didn't know what to say. She didn't know why she was here. Fake white marble columns stood sentry beside open, wrought iron gates. They walked in along a graveled path, leading to a startling green meadow speared by tombstones. The bag lady marched across the grass.

"Wait," Laurel called. "You're walking on graves."

"They're all dead anyway, they don't know I'm here," she said. Laurel followed her, dodging areas obviously occupied. The bag lady walked resolutely onward. Laurel caught up with her at an open patch of grass.

"This is it," the bag lady said. "This here tree is an ash. I asked for that. Reminds me of Virginia. That's where I'm from." The tree was still small and scraggly, and spread only a feathered pattern over the gravesite.

"You shouldn't come out here so much," Laurel said. "It's morbid. What do you care where your body will rest? You, the real you, will be dead. Grass and trees won't matter."

"You an atheist?" the bag lady asked. "You was the one afraid of waking the dead walking over here. Ain't it nice and peaceful here? That's what I care about. Rest for my weary bones. And this is where I want to rest." She pulled a bunch of wilted daisies out of her shopping bag and laid them on the grass. "I told 'em I want fresh daisies on my grave every week."

They walked slowly back to the gate.

"You gonna order one?" the bag lady asked.

"Oh, I will, but not today. I left my checkbook at home."

"You better hurry up before they raise the price any," the bag lady said. "Now we have to wait half an hour for the dad burn bus."

"Would you like to go somewhere and have a cup of coffee?" Laurel asked her.

"You buying?"

"Of course," Laurel said. Then she looked up and down the empty street and yelled, "Taxi! Taxi! Taxi!"

The next day she stayed home, weeding her small garden of tomatoes, squash, and strawberries. She couldn't risk running into the bag lady again. They had finally gone into the office at the graveyard to call for a taxi, and Laurel had bought her coffee at the little restaurant around the corner from the Acacia Hotel. Actually, it had been more than coffee, as the woman wanted a sweet roll to go along with the coffee, and a bowl of strawberries and whipped cream to go along with the sweet roll. Laurel had paid the check and left her there, scooping the last of the whipped cream out of the bowl with careful deliberation. How do I get myself into these messes, Laurel wondered. All I wanted to do was ride the buses around town, minding my own business. I don't even want to think about people like her, much less spend time with them. It's too late for me to do anything about all the poverty and misery in the world. The only charity I have left is for myself.

She stayed off the buses for a week, visiting several new restaurants with Lucy and scrubbing and polishing her hardwood floors. She knew they must be dirty, even though she couldn't see the spots anymore. She still cared enough to present a clean house inside, even if it was too late for neighborhood competition outside.

On Monday she had to buy groceries, so she walked to the Wasatch bus stop and waited. It would be stretching the possibilities of coincidence for the bag lady to be on this bus, Laurel thought. When it pulled up and the doors opened, she poked her head in first to check the opposite seat. No one was there. She climbed aboard to assume her own seat. At the store she bought her few groceries carefully, knowing just how much would fill the one sack she could carry. The return bus was empty, and she rode home, tired and alone.

The next day she took a tour bus out to the Air Force Academy, to see what the military was up to. The last time she'd been out there was to see a play the faculty drama club presented, a very tame version of "Little Foxes." Life in the military did nothing to nurture the unbridled emotion necessary to portray a Birdie or Regina, she decided. Now she saw cadets marching across the fields, running to class, and sitting ramrod straight in an antiseptic cafeteria where they served the bus passengers mottled meat loaf and soggy peas.

When the bus returned to the terminal, instead of transferring to the Weber line for home, she walked the few blocks to the Acacia Hotel. Inside, at the desk, she realized she didn't know the bag lady's name.

"Excuse me," she said to the clerk. "I'm looking for one of your residents, but I don't know her name."

"Is that right," the man said. "That leaves me about sixty people out of a hundred, since at least you say it's a 'she'."

"I'm sorry," Laurel said. "I can describe her for you."

"Yeah, she's old, she has gray hair, and she walks with a cane," he said.

"Excuse me, but you don't have to be so sarcastic," Laurel said. "Nobody can help being old."

"Okay, lady, describe who you're looking for and I'll see what I can do."

"She always wears a wool hat pulled down over her ears and rubber boots."

"Why didn't you say so in the first place," he said. "That's crazy Mary. She lives in Room 48."

"Do you know if she's in?" Laurel asked.

"As a matter of fact, I haven't seen her yet this morning. She's usually up and out by eight. She always tells me she's got 'important things to do today.' I'm glad somebody thinks they're important."

"Thank you," Laurel said, and took the elevator to the fourth floor. Room 48 was in an alcove at the end of the hall. Laurel knocked on the door. Just as she was about to knock again, the door inched open. The bag lady's crunched up face peered through the crack.

"Mary, it's me," Laurel said.

"What are you doing here, and how do you know my name's Mary?" the bag lady said.

"I came to visit you," Laurel said. "The man at the desk told me your name and room number. May I come in?"

"What for?" Lucy asked.

"I came to visit you," Laurel repeated.

"Nosy busybody, ain't you," Lucy said as she opened the door.

Laurel entered the room. That's all it was, one shabby room with a bed, miniature stove and refrigerator, a few pieces of miscellaneous furniture, and plastic shopping bags everywhere. The most startling thing about the room was Mary. She was still dressed in cardigan sweater and rubber boots, but the hat was missing. Tiny wisps of yellowish colored hair stood straight up from an almost bald head. Oh no, thought Laurel, she's sweated so much she's lost her hair.

"I'm usually out of here by now," Mary said. "I've always got things to do."

"I'm glad I caught you then. I wanted to come by and see you and invite you to my house for dinner."

"I told you, I'm always out by now, but today I'm not because my arthritis is kicking up and if I ain't up to doing the things I have to do I definitely ain't up to going to some stranger's house for dinner. You go around inviting all the Acacia charity cases to your house to dinner so you don't feel so guilty about being rich?"

"I'm not rich, Mary," Laurel said. "You know, you shouldn't be so ornery. I invited you to dinner because I think you're an interesting person and I'd like to know more about you."

"You some kind of psychiatrist for the feeble?" Mary said. "Only I ain't feeble. I mind my own business and expect others to mind theirs."

Laurel lost her tempter. "All right, Mary, if you want to be nasty, that's your business. But don't tell me to mind my own business when you're the one who's so nosy. I could have told you it was none of your damn business when you wanted to know if I had a funeral plan or not. Talk about wanting to know something that's none of your business."

"What's so private about dying, lady?" Lucy asked. "We're all going to go sooner or later."

"My name is Laurel, not lady," Laurel said. "And dying is the most intensely private and personal thing anyone does. And I'm glad I'm going to face it with a little more sensitivity than you seem capable of."

"You one of those death with dignity nuts?" Mary asked. "There ain't nothing dignified about watching your skin crinkle and sag, your arteries choke, your joints turn to cellophane, and your ticker run out of octane. You got some stupid notion that when your time comes you're gonna rise up and face your maker with peace plastered on your face and serenity guarding your soul? Well, lady, I'll bet you'll be lying there screaming along with the rest of them, 'Why me? Why me?'"

"And I suppose you'll be lying there stoically saying, 'Come and get me, I'm yours.'"

"I don't believe in no God coming to get me," Mary said. "But I ain't afraid of the undertaker."

"Won't you reconsider and come to my house for dinner?" Laurel asked.

"I told you my arthritis is kicking up and I ain't going nowhere. I can't even climb up the steps of the dad burned bus."

"I'll come get you in my car, Mary. You won't have to ride the bus."

"You got a car, lady?"

"Laurel. My name is Laurel. Yes, I have a car. I'll come get you this evening at five o'clock. That will give you some time to rest and take care of your arthritis."

Before Mary could answer, Laurel was out of her room and hurrying down the stairs. What do I have in the refrigerator that I can make for dinner, she thought. She tried not to think about getting the car out of the garage and negotiating the driveway backwards.

At four-thirty, Laurel knocked on her neighbor's door and asked him to please back her car out of the garage and into the street. He was a young architect who lived in an apartment behind his office, and helped her with various chores around her house, including driving her car into the garage.

"Are you sure you can still drive?" he asked politely. "I wouldn't want you to get hurt or anything."

"I only have trouble going backwards and turning," Laurel said. "All I have to do is drive straight down Weber to the Acacia, turn around once, and drive straight back. I'll leave the car parked at the curb, and maybe in the morning you could put it in the garage for me."

"I'd be happy to," he said. "Would you like me to drive you down to the Acacia?"

"No, no thank you. I'm going to have enough trouble getting Mary in the car without some nice, good looking young man in there, too."

He looked at her perplexed but backed the car out of the garage and left it idling in the street.

She drove down Weber in the center lane, avoiding the parked cars, and pulled into the U-shaped driveway of the Acacia. The sign there said she had five minutes to complete her business before she got towed away.

Mary was there, in the lobby, complete with wool hat and boots.

"Oh, you're here, Mary, I'm so glad," Laurel said, guiding her out to the car.

"No sense fighting a losing battle," Mary said.

Laurel settled Mary in the passenger's seat and negotiated the turn out of the driveway back onto Weber. Luckily there was little traffic, and she pulled up to the curb opposite her house. She went around and opened the door for Mary.

"You're as bad as the bus drivers," Lucy said, noting the two-foot gap between car and curb. "You inviting some car to come by and sideswipe you?"

"It's all right, Mary, it's a quiet street," Laurel said.

Inside, Mary shed only her vest and walked around the living room staring at all Laurel's possessions.

"Would you like a drink, Mary? Dinner will be ready in about half an hour."

"What you got?" Mary asked.

"I could make you a nice martini, or scotch and water, or maybe you'd prefer a glass of wine?"

"I don't drink," Mary said. "Been on the wagon for twenty years."

"Oh," Laurel said. "In that case, I'll just go get dinner ready."

In the kitchen she quickly mixed herself a martini and hid it behind the toaster. She went to the door and peaked around the corner at Mary, who had moved from the living room to dining room and was examining each of the little miniatures Laurel had collected in her old printer's letterbox. Please don't let her break any, Laurel prayed.

She had dinner on the table as soon as possible. Mary didn't say anything as she chomped on chicken bones and stuffed her mouth with broccoli. When she came up for air she said, "You ain't as rich as I thought you'd be."

"I told you I wasn't rich," Laurel said. "Would you care for some French bread?"

"Yeah, tear me off a piece. I get the day old loaves of that stuff down at the bakery for half price. I guess if you can afford it fresh you're rich enough."

"What kind of work did you do when you were younger, Mary?" Laurel asked.

"How come houses are always so full of junk?" Mary asked, chewing her French bread. "Everybody spends half their life collecting all this stuff to sit on shelves and collect dust and then it has to be carted away to the dump when they die."

Laurel tried again. "Do you have any children, Mary?"

"Kids come in after their parents die and fight over who's gonna get which piece of junk to take home and clutter up their own house. I spent all my life getting down to the essentials, and when I go out to Memorial Gardens all that's gonna be left of me is my social security number."

"I want my children to have all my things," Laurel said. "They've meant a lot to me over the years. You can't live on bread alone."

"Reminders of days gone by, that's all," Mary said. "What's for dessert?"

Laurel got up and went to the kitchen. She took some chocolate ice cream out of the freezer and dished two bowls, one twice the size of the other. Over the large dish she dumped a quarter of a can of chocolate syrup.

Mary ate the ice cream with gusto. When she was finished, she went into the living room, put on her vest and announced, "Thanks for dinner. You got a bus token?"

"I'll take you home," Laurel said. "The car is already in the street, after all."

"That's why I think I'll take the bus," Mary said.

"I'll walk you to the bus, then," Laurel said, relieved.

Mary shrugged her shoulders. "I never expected anything better."

They walked to the bus stop in silence.

"Here's a bus token," Laurel said, as the bus pulled up.

Mary took it. "That saves me both of mine today." She climbed up the stairs and took her seat. As the bus pulled away, she called through the open window, "See you on the buses, lady."

"I guess you probably will," Laurel laughed softly, "but please, God, lay me down anywhere but Memorial Gardens." Then she slowly walked home.

Slimy Devils

Every now and again one gets disgusted with men and calls it quits. You think you've found one who's honest and true, then he lets you in on the joke that all's not fair, period. So you leave him and go crawl away somewhere until you can look at a man again and he's not wearing two horns and a tail and covered in slime.

I crawled into this place in Alamita with no indoor toilet but a nice shower and bath, and with my son Adam, a beautiful kid. He's the son of a slimy devil, but I don't hold that against him. When his father came over one night, camped in my front yard and threatened to stay until I agreed to let him back in my bed, Adam took his sleeping bag out and played gin rummy with him until he went home.

My neighbors are the Gonzales family. They have seven children who all look like Mr. Gonzales, a burly little man, and live in cinder block houses behind their parents. Adam loves the Gonzales's and spends most of his time over there, as I have to go up to the free-form and drill heishi every day. Drilling heishi is no fun, to say the least. And the freeform, despite its consoling name, is just as bad. It's this place up the highway from Alamita, made from leftovers, a double meaning of free. Some of these leftovers are tire rims, which comprise the rafters, and beer bottles, which comprise the walls. The whole thing has been sprayed with foam insulation so it looks like an ocean sponge transplanted to the desert.

Inside the freeform are the drills, all lined up against the beer bottle walls, waiting for us to plug them in and drill, drill, drill until our thumbs are numb and our minds catatonic. Our thumbs get numb because in order to drill heishi, which are little bits of shell that will be strung together and ground down into smooth, beautiful necklaces, one has to hold the heishi with tweezers. Holding tweezers for more than an hour is painful. But it's all for a buck, and a pretty easy one at that as heishi necklaces are the rage right now and hippie entrepreneurs say they're only expanding the market for the Indians who've been making the necklaces for hundreds of years. It's keeping Adam and me off welfare at least.

Living in Alamita with me is a woman named Julie. She's a masseuse, which is the best kind of roommate to have. She likes to practice on us, to get her fingers going for her weekdays at the spa. Knowing how I feel about men right now she assures me that the only ones there with their clothes off are the customers, and all intimate details are discreetly toweled. "Besides," she says, "I've never particularly liked the way men's bodies look, just what they can do with them. And I keep them well tuned so they can keep on doing it."

Julie's not mad at men at all. She's that type of person whose sense of self is so finally chiseled and hewn that no one, especially a man, would dare disregard it. Whenever I ask her what the secret is, she says it's no secret, it's strategy, and some of us are better planners than others. The way I see it, Julie's arrived while I'm still stumbling along the path to nowhere. She currently has this boyfriend named Jason, but she always sleeps with him at his house, and he takes Adam fishing sometimes, so I get along with him all right.

One day Julie gives Adam and me free passes for a day's session at the spa. Since Adam is not particularly keen on Jacuzzis and would rather play with Moises Gonzales, I ask Moises's mother if she'd like to go with me instead.

"Do they make men and women use the same facilities?" she asks me. "You know, I've had seven children and I sag a little."

"You're probably in better shape than half the people there, Mrs. Gonzales," I say. "But I think everything is separate except the swimming pool. We can just go and lie in the Jacuzzi and soak our tired bones and then have Julie give us a massage."

"Oh, it sounds so nice," Mrs. Gonzales says. "I can't swim anyway. I fell down in the Rio Grande once and almost drowned."

So we go on down to the spa and Mrs. Gonzales is absolutely astounded by the squirting jets of water attacking her body in the Jacuzzi.

"Forgive my blasphemy, but this is heaven," she says.

"I think I'll go swim some laps and then come back for some more later," I say. "I'm not quite ready to be Jacuzzied to jelly."

Everything at the spa is plastic and perfect and exceedingly claustrophobic, especially the swimming pool. Frog-like people in white bathing caps and goggles swim back and forth and back and forth with slow, methodical strokes that seem barely able to keep them afloat. I dive in and do two lengths of butterfly, to assure myself that I'm still alive and to relive the days when swimming competitively gave me something to live for. I've splashed water into the faces of my neighboring swimmers, and one woman is standing in the shallow end choking, so I slow down to the breaststroke, and join the ranks of swimmers swimming back and forth, back and forth. I used to do this for hours as a kid, toning my muscles to beat my opponents in a furor of competitive bliss, but now it's just boring, so I climb out of the pool.

An Adonis type speaks to me as I am pulling at my suit to hide my no longer well-toned muscles.

"I saw you do those laps of butterfly," he says. "I'll bet you used to race."

"Strictly a breaststroker," I say. "No endurance."

"I did individual medley myself," he says. He looks like he's a weight lifter to me. Muscles bulge like popcorn balls all over his body.

"Are you a member of the spa?" he asks. "I've never seen you here before."

"Just a friend of the masseuse," I say. "I'm not interested in developing popcorn balls."

"You're a friend of Julie's!" he says, grinning. "She gives me a rub down every Monday morning and keeps me going for the rest of the week. What a woman."

What a man, I think. He's probably wanted her for weeks; now's his chance to zero in.

"Excuse me, but I have a rendezvous with Mrs. Gonzales in the Jacuzzi."

"Say hi to Julie for me," he says. "My name's Sam."

"Right-oh, Sam," I say. "My name's Victim—Victim of Slimy Devils."

Mrs. Gonzales is still there in the Jacuzzi with her eyes closed, dreaming about heaven, maybe. I get in and dream with her.

"I wish Willie could be here," she says to me, wiping the sweat from her forehead. "He works so hard, and it would help his leg."

"I've noticed that Mr. Gonzales walks with a limp," I say politely. "Was he involved in an accident?"

"One day the tree behind our house started to fall down and Willy held it up until me and the kids got out of the way. Then it fell on him and broke his leg."

Although I don't doubt Mrs. Gonzales' veracity, I find this an incredible story. But then I've never found Mr. Gonzales to be particularly slimy, either. Obviously Mrs. Gonzales doesn't.

We go into the massage room, and I lie under Julie's hands, which slap, stretch, and pull me until I'm a quivering mass of jelly.

"Mr. Adonis says hello," I mumble, my mouth squashed to the table.

"You mean Sam?" Julie says, pulling on my toes until each one resoundingly snaps. "I give him his weekly massage today. Man, I love working on that body. He's the Maserati of mankind—balanced and aligned. Very polite, too. Never made a pass at me in two years."

"Poor repressed sonofabitch," I say.

"Not necessarily," Julie says. "Maybe I'm not his type."

"If you're not, I can't imagine who is. Maybe he likes men."

"I doubt it," Julie says, cracking my back one last time. "He's too polite. Women are obviously lovers, not comrades."

Adam's father comes over to pick him up on weekends. I usually hide in the bedroom, taking a nap or pretending to, until they're gone. But today a stray dog starts chasing the chickens, and I'm outside with a bucket of water chasing the dog.

"Why are you trying to give that dog a bath?" he calls after me, leaning on his car, drinking a beer.

"Very funny," I say, throwing the water, missing the dog by a mile. "You could have helped, you know."

"You seem to have the situation under control. Just like always."

"You never know when to quit, do you?" I say.

"And you can't take a joke, can you?"

Adam appears, interrupting our crap.

"Dad, we going fishing? Should I bring my gear?" His question is filled with hopefulness, and his dad hears it.

"Sure, why not. We can go up to Fenton Lake and be back before dinner. We're going over to the Marley's for dinner."

"Are you going to take the boat up?" I ask. "If you do make sure Adam wears his vest." I've never felt anyone could care for Adam as well as I—even his dad. Not a good assumption in the game of marriage. I lost points on that one. This time he lets it slide by. We're not keeping score anymore.

"The Marley's said to say hello," he says.

"I haven't seen them in months," I say. "I guess we know whose friends they turned out to be."

"You're perfectly capable of stopping by to see them, you know," he says. "You don't have to play the pariah down here in this dump."

"They were only friendly with me because I was your wife. I could never hold up my end of the conversation anyway. But then competing with your mouth was never an easy task."

"You are really fucked up," he says. "Tell Adam to hurry up."

"Please have Adam back by Sunday afternoon," I say. "We're supposed to be in town by seven."

"Got a date?" he asks.

"You've got to be kidding," I say.

"Oh, yeah, I forgot. You've taken us all to task for my sins. You'll get over it when you get horny enough."

"Do all men think that's the solution to everything?"

"No, but most of us know that you ain't got much without it. But then that was the way you liked things—sexless."

"I just found out I didn't enjoy fucking someone I hated."

"Yeah, the best tool in your war of destruction."

Adam comes out of the house with his gear. I kiss him goodbye, and they are gone. I breathe a sigh of despair.

On Monday I'm lying in a stupor on the couch after four hours of drilling. Julie comes home and says Sam asked her if she thought it would be all right if he came over to visit me.

"Did you tell him I don't associate with slimy devils right now?" I say.

"Maggie," Julie says.

From the tone of her voice I deduce that Julie's patience is wearing thin. Have I crossed the line where my mania ceases to be amusing? She'd probably like to tell me to stop feeling so sorry for myself, to get on with my life. She probably thinks she'd tell me this because she hates seeing me so unhappy and listless. But really it's because things aren't funny anymore, and she's right. I'm beginning to bore myself. But I still can't get rid of the image.

Apparently Julie's plan of attack is to ignore my wishes and to tell Sam to come by because that's just what he does.

"Couldn't get your butterfly off my mind," he says to me.

"It's such an important skill to have," I say.

"Don't knock it, you might as well capitalize on what you've got. It impressed me, didn't it?"

Adam walks into the room and I introduce them.

"I met your mom at the spa. She was splashing all the water out of the pool doing the butterfly," Sam says.

"What's that?" Adam asks.

"Adam doesn't get to go swimming very often," I say. "Not too many YMCA's in Alamita."

"I've got an idea," Sam says. "Let's drive out to Cochiti Lake and I'll teach Adam the butterfly."

"What's the butterfly?" Adam asks again.

"Go show Sam your rabbits and then we'll go out to the lake and you'll see," I say.

They go off, and I put on my sexiest bathing suit. In the mirror I look like mush, as opposed to slime.

Going to Cochiti on a hundred degree day is not one of the smartest things to do. Cochiti Lake is this manmade reservoir leased from Cochiti Pueblo where wealthy white folks have built lakeshore houses and can sail their boats in the middle of the desert. On the public beach at Cochiti there are no trees, there are rocks instead of sand, and the water is murky green laced with opaque brown. We all go and sit in the water to avoid sunstroke.

"Show Adam the butterfly," Sam says to me.

"I think my suit will fall off if I try it. You show him."

Sam jumps up out of the water into a leaping dive. He comes up butterflying away.

"You're kidding," Adam says. "I can't do that.

He swims off with a sloppy front crawl, kicking his feet as hard as he can to emphasize his point. When his head pops up twenty feet away, Sam comes up next to him with a few long strokes. They swim off together towards the boat dock, Sam coaxing him along with gentle instruction.

I crawl out of the water to go lie in the sun and burn awhile. Two men are throwing a Frisbee over me, a couple is making out on a blanket next to me, and a dog is chasing spiders around me. I'm soon hypnotized by the blue intensity of the New Mexico sky. I've never seen sky this color anywhere else. It's part of the romance of this place I've chosen to call home:

limitless expanse of sapphire sky canopied over red mesas, green dotted hills of piñon pine and alligator junipers, miles of sand and rock and sage and rabbit brush, the backdrop to these scenes of color and contrast. It's addictive, this southwestern landscape—like they say about getting high, enhancing perceptions, crystallizing images. Slimy devils run rampant in New Mexico.

Just as I'm dozing off, Sam and Adam shake water all over me and collapse in giggles on the rocks. I'm glad someone is having a good time.

"You're getting burned, Mom," Adam says.

"Well, I can't sit in the water all day, can I?"

"Put your shirt on," he says, and jumps up to catch a Frisbee. He runs off to join their game.

Sam stretches out on the towel next to me and says, "You're funny."

"Adam is actually a very nice child when he isn't acting like my mother," I say sitting up, wrapping my towel across my burned shoulders.

"I think Adam is a great kid despite his having to act like your mother when you start acting like his kid."

"Well," I say, in my best Bette Davis pose. "Presumptuous sonofabitch, aren't you?"

"I'm not going to get mad at you no matter how nasty you are to me," Sam says. "And no matter how hard you try to see my slime, my will keeps the vision dispelled."

"What are you talking about?" I ask, nonchalantly.

"Julie told me. Slimy devils are a dime a dozen. So are witches. All depends on what you want."

"Don't give me that crap about it takes two to tango, or deserving what you get. Nobody deserves slimy devils."

"Life ain't a bed of roses, either, if you want to toss around some corny clichés. You ever seen a major league baseball player get one strike against him, throw down his bat and ball and quit the game?"

"Oh, for God's sake, shut-up," I say. "I'm going out to swim some butterfly."

This guy thinks he's very clever, I say to myself as I wade into the water. I don't trust him an inch. I don't trust any of them an inch. Men and women make a terrible combination. They always have and they always will. Men will always like men better than women, and women will always like women better than men. And they'll never be sympathetic to each other because they can never understand what could possibly have motivated the other to do what he or she is doing to create the situation that calls for the sympathy. One is a dog and one is a cat; they may lie down together occasionally, but it's unnatural.

I should know. My husband and I tried to lie down together for five years. The only thing we produced besides Adam was enough hostility to kill any semblance of sympathy. Not only are men and women bad combinations, a man and a woman together, alone, is impossible. When he'd tell me I was a castrating bitch, I believed him. When I told him he was immature and worthless, who else did he have to tell him otherwise?

We started out all right, just like everyone does. He was from the East, I was from the West, and everyone said we were the perfect American Yin and Yang. My earthiness balanced his vitality. But somewhere along the line admired traits turn tortuous. When your companion has to be everything you aren't, relentlessly, vitality and earthiness lose their mystique. Then the dog and the cat resort to primitive behavior, and war is declared.

I lost. On either front, physical or mental, I was out maneuvered. I'm not saying he beat me up—verbal abuse was nasty enough. He was tougher, that's all. I admit it. But if men take pride in their ability to inflict pain, that's their problem. I just wish I'd known enough to stay out of the way. I know now.

The water reaches my waist, and I throw myself in and come up butterflying through the air in exhilaration. I hope he's watching.

That night the Gonzales's have a barbecue, so we go on over. I introduce Sam to Mr. Gonzales and they immediately have a conversation about foundations and stem walls. I'm helping Mrs. Gonzales spread chile on the hamburger buns when Julie comes up, smiling.

"Did you have fun at the lake?"

"I got burned."

"You went out to Cochiti today?" Mrs. Gonzales asks. "I hear it's lovely out there."

"If you like lots of hot rocks and screaming people, it's okay," I say. She's never been there. She's probably never been to Bandelier or Canyon de Chelly or Jemez Falls, either, any of the places all of us who weren't born here go like pilgrims to acquaint ourselves with the wonders of our adopted home. She mourns never seeing Cochiti Lake, or any city bigger than El Paso;

I mourn never seeing Florence or Nepal. Is that why I see slimy devils and she sees her husband for life, Mr. Gonzales?

"Sam and Adam seem to have hit it off," Julie says biting into a hamburger.

"All right, all right," I say "we had a good time out at the lake and I'm having a good time at the barbecue, but just don't make anything more out of this, okay, Julie?"

"Listen, Maggie, I..." Julie begins.

"I'm sorry," I interrupt. "You're not the one I'm mad at. Men are insidious."

"It's your reaction to them that's insidious," Julie says. "Mrs. Gonzales, don't you agree that one must appreciate the difference between them and us, and love them for that difference?"

"Julie is right, dear," Mrs. Gonzales says to me, putting a hamburger in my bun. "Willie and I've been married for thirty years and he still won't go to confession."

Sam comes over and shares his beer with me, until it's time to take Adam inside and put him to bed.

"How's your sunburn, Mom?"

"Okay, how's your tolerance for your dumb old Mom?"

"You're not so old," Adam says with a grin.

"Thanks, I needed that."

"I'm glad to have met you, Adam," Sam says.

"See you around, Sam," Adam says.

We go and sit in the living room, and I can't think of a thing to say. He has no trouble at all.

"Well, I had a real nice day, and I meant what I said about being glad to have met Adam, he's a great kid, and the Gonzales's are wonderful people. He's done everything and knows everything there is to know about adobe building. I think we should drive up to the Jemez tomorrow where it's cooler."

"How can you be like this?" I ask, astounded. "How can you be so enthusiastic about everything? I can't be that way. I just get lost in the shuffle."

"Does this make you feel less lost?" he asks, pushing back my hair and planting a kiss on my neck.

"A little bit," I say.

"There's more," he says, taking off my blouse. "The best part."

In the morning Adam is in the kitchen when Sam and I appear.

"There's no milk, Mom," Adam says, looking at Sam.

"Run next door and get a quart of goat's milk from Mrs. Gonzales, would you, honey?" I say.

"Okay," Adam says. "Do you like goat's milk, Sam?"

"Sure, as long as the billy goat's not living in the same quarters as the momma goat. Males have a way of smelling up an otherwise nice arrangement."

"Was that remark directed at me?" I ask, incredulously, as soon as Adam is out the door. "I wouldn't dream of presuming that our night of sex was anything more than that. You're the one who made the pass, and you're the one who wanted to go to Jemez today."

"Touchy, aren't you, my dear," he says, putting his arms around me. "I was referring to male goats, although there are some masculine traits that cross species barriers. Not all of us fuck for love."

My heart drops to my toes. I know I am being told, diplomatically, of course, that the pursuance is over. Apparently I am considered won. Is this the end of the game? I take three deep breaths, kiss him on the cheek, and move out of his slippery arms.

"I know Adam will be disappointed, but I'm afraid we can't go to Jemez with you. I forgot I have a dentist appointment tomorrow. Bad gums."

"Oh, too bad, but we can go some other time. I'd like to get my fishing gear together anyway, so Adam and I can catch some big ones. Does he have a reel?"

"Yes, his dad is a great fisherman."

"Great. I'll call next weekend, and we can take our gear and camp out at the falls. How does that sound?"

"Lovely," I say, mechanically measuring out coffee grounds.

"Now what's for breakfast?" he asks.

He's gone in an hour, and I go lie down on my crumpled bed. Adam is on the phone with his father, after a quick conversation with me about the necessity of Dad's exclusion from my life and any gossip theretofore related. I am devastated. Why should I have supposed he had any interest in me beyond his male preoccupation with seduction? But why are they always so insistent on separating sex and love? I can't anymore. I'm too old. He never even gave me a chance. Not that I wanted one from him anyway, but I want to be the one who declares that, not him. Oh, why did I let those popcorn balls distract me?

Maybe I'm overreacting. Maybe he's more fucked up than me, masking fear with bravado and that crap about goats. But I can't control the sinking pit of my stomach, where the murky suspicions of male culpability are lodged. One night of sex, no matter how nice, can't be worth it. I roll over and cry into wet, smelly sheets.

Julie comes home from Jason's while I'm washing the dishes.

"When I saw Sam's car and your closed bedroom door last night I went over to Jason's," she says, giving me a quick hug. "I bet he's incredible in bed."

I immediately burst into tears.

"What's the matter, babe?" she asks, consolingly. "Here, sit down and tell me about it."

I can't say a word.

"Was he a lousy lay?" she asks.

I only cry harder.

"Impotent?"

I shake my head vigorously.

"You had a good time together in bed?"

I nod my head just as vigorously."

"Well, let's see then. He didn't say anything about coming over to see you again?"

"No," I wailed. "I'm the one who told him I was busy today, and he asked us to go camping next weekend."

"Then what is going on, my dear?" Julie asks. "I thought Sam would be just what you needed."

"Yeah, to prove he was desirable to someone who sees slimy devils. I was the ultimate conquest of Mr. Adonis. No wonder he went for me instead of you—he knew he could never pull anything over on you. But on Ms. Paranoia herself the sky was the limit."

"How did you deduce all this?"

"He said not all men fuck for love."

"I should hope not," Julie says. "There would be a lot of horny people in this world, if that were the case."

"I know he was telling me that this was strictly for kicks, a challenge, not a sign of any kind of affection."

"But he wants to see you again?"

"So he says. I know now he's just another slimy devil."

Julie sighs. "You obviously were not quite ready for this. The opposite of slimy devil isn't Prince Charming, you know. No reason to believe he exists either, Maggie. They're just men, that's all."

So maybe I am getting carried away. Maybe my mind is still muddled with too much grease and slime. But I tell you, this sexual dilemma between men and women is debilitating, when all anyone wants (or what they should want) is a little uncomplicated love and affection. No such luck, I guess. I wish Adam didn't have to go through it. Will my son make women cry and weep?

Sam calls on Friday and we go camping Saturday. By Sunday I've decided he's pretentious, pompous, and superficial. I especially don't like the way he spends five minutes washing each dish with biodegradable soap as soon as Adam and I set them down. When he tells me he'll call, I tell him I'll call him.

"Did you have fun this weekend with Sam?" I ask Adam on Monday, as I prepare to go drill heishi.

"He's okay," Adam says. "Except he doesn't know as much as Dad about fishing."

"I don't think I'm going to see him anymore," I say.

"Why not?" Adam asks. "He's okay to go camping with."

"Well, maybe I can find someone else who'll go camping with us. Someone who likes dirty plates."

"You're the boss," Adam laughs, flipping up my hair as he goes out the door.

What a darling child I have, I think, as I look at myself closely in the mirror for the first time in six months. I can't really tell if I've taken one step forward or two steps back, but if I can find my face again, the mush of my features must be settling somewhat into place. Now if I could just do something about all the slimy devils.

Our Heart and Soul

It's strange to see how all your friends' kids turn out. You know the parents—all their quirks, foibles, talents, history—but you never seem to know them so well that their kids' choices in life aren't a big shock. Like the Covingtons. Here are two parents, writers, whose house practically falls down around them because of no left brain while their son Gus can put a completely dismantled truck back together in a week. The fact that he's never read William Carlos Williams or Melville disgruntles them no end, but at least he's handy around the house.

I guess because we dragged our kids everywhere with us when they were little we expected them to be more like us. They fell asleep on beds at parties, in the car on the ride home from Indian dances or craft fairs, in backpacks on hikes in the mountains, in strange beds in strange towns all over America while we played out our nomadic angst.

The Ashleys were the only ones who ever attempted to have "adults only" parties. They'd clear out the living room, assemble all their New Orleans music, and expect us to arrive childless and ready to dance. Even though it was wonderful to dance and drink and smoke pot unobserved, some of us actually bristled a little at the idea of a party with no kids. Did Leland and Ellen Ashley secretly dislike kids, despite having two of their own? Did they secretly dislike our kids, and think they were obnoxious? Were we being too bourgeois, like our parents, leaving our kids home?

"For God's sake, we need a break from our kids sometimes," Ellen said when she called to announce their latest party the following Saturday.

"I know," I said, "but the only people my kids ever stay with are going to be at the party, too. I don't have a real baby sitter."

"I don't either, but thank God, Leland's parents are in town and the kids are with them at their motel telling all kinds of wicked stories about us no doubt. Find some fourteen-year old desperate for money to buy paint thinner or something, but don't miss this party. If anyone brings their kids I'm going to lock them in Quentin and Delia's room and feed them spiked Twinkies."

We all somehow managed to comply with Ellen and Leland's dictate—our own kids were transported down the hill to stay-at-home-friends in Alamita—and Saturday's party was duly wild and wonderful. Ellen and Leland were also the only couple in Rositas who ever stocked a full bar at parties. Southern hospitality had its charms.

"My parents would pervert my children instantaneously if I let them see them more than once a year," Leland said, as we danced to the Wild Tchoupitoulas. "They're hideous people."

"Worried about tonight? Delia and Quentin are tough kids," I assured him.

"One can never be tough enough when confronted with the decadence of the Ashley clan, Southern inbred gentry par excellence," he said, jumping into the air and coming down red-faced. "But tonight we dance away our genes, we discard our heritage, we rejoice in ourselves as individuals—parentless, childless, spouseless." And he grabbed my ass.

I moved away to dance with my husband.

"I saw Leland grab your ass," Ben said.

"That's as far as it ever goes," I laughed. "He'd never make a move without consulting Ellen first."

Leland and Ellen's children, Delia and Quentin, were the serious, quiet types who spent their childhoods counterbalancing their parents' inspired neuroses. As with Gus Covington, however, we were all in for a big surprise fifteen years later. The Ashleys left Rositas when the children entered puberty, to enroll them in private schools and settle into East coast gentility. We all kept in touch, sporadically, by letters and occasional visits. After a gap of several years of no news, however, we were sent a newspaper clipping of Quentin standing in front of a sculpture he had just completed called "The Eroticism of Pat Nixon." A handwritten note at the bottom of the clipping said, "We attended Quentin's opening with Delia, whom we hadn't seen in two years. She's currently a nightclub dancer in Spokane."

We all moved out onto the Ashley's deck as the sun descended and the high desert night air brought relief. The deck provided a great vantage point for viewing the mountains that defined the southern boundary of Rositas. I often wondered that so many of my neighbors' experience of these mountains, so close to our lives, was only that—a great view.

Not so the son of Carp Kalistad, however, who stood by the railing quenching his endless thirst for beer. A tall, rangy kid built just like his six-foot-four dad, Sonny Kalistad (named for Sonny Boy Williamson) knew every nook and cranny in those mountains. Disdainful of trails, Sonny would take off on a summer morning with his water bottle and knapsack and not return home until after dark.

"Scaled North Peak today, Dad," he would announce to Carp. "Found a new route without ropes."

His dad joined him when he could, but a thriving cabinet making business kept him home most days. Various girlfriends kept him busy at night. Sonny was raised on a diet of blues, beer, hard work, and overnight women, but when the time came to break away from Carp's version of the good life, he couldn't. After an extra year of high school, another year of job hunting, and a final year of threats and recriminations, Carp accompanied Sonny to the Army recruiters and he was gone, finally, to West Germany.

"Carp, how could you?" I asked. "You were a conscientious objector to the Viet Nam war."

"I couldn't get that kid off his butt," Carp said. "I couldn't get him to have a life."

"You didn't fall for that 'Join the Army and get educated' crap, did you? They still educate to kill, you know."

"Nah, I fell for the 'Join the Army and get some discipline in your life,'" Carp said. "Sonny has to get out of bed every morning now."

"Heard from him lately?" I asked.

"Yeah, the kid went and married a German hausfrau," Carp said. "The baby's due in October."

"Sounds like once he got off his butt he did so with a vengeance. How's he planning on supporting a wife and kid?"

"He reenlisted," Carp said. "Gets to paint airplanes for two more years."

After two margaritas and a few unadorned shots of tequila, I was forced to sit on the deck steps and watch the other dancers. We were truly children of the sixties, here in the late seventies, nurturing our membership in that unique history despite our children, regular jobs, and home ownership. We looked the part, too. Carp's hair touched his waist in a ponytail. Ellen Ashley wore Guatemalan skirts while Leland wore muslin. Susan and Sam Covington, Gus's parents, lived in a triple dome with wood heat and an occasional baby goat. Ben and I lived in our handmade adobe with resurrected school house lights and windows.

Laura, my best friend, was perhaps the loveliest of all out there, swaying to the strains of Gimme Shelter. With long, curly, dark hair and wicked eyes, she was always the life of these parties. The bane of her existence, however, was her fatherless child Max. The product of her one-year marriage at age nineteen, Max, at seven, was smart, independent, and definitely noncompliant. Besides the fact that he was always there, to be taken care of, nurtured, related to, when Laura was mainly interested in enjoying her youth and the excitement of the times.

Ben and I thought Max was a great kid, but of course we didn't have to be his parents. One time we met Laura, Max, and Laura's latest boyfriend at the Telluride Jazz Festival high in the San Juan Mountains of Colorado. Laura, Max, and Neal, the boyfriend, left Rositas several days before the festival to secure a campsite in the city park, next to the festival stage (these were the days before the yuppies took over Telluride and the rich were the only ones who could afford tickets). Ben and I arrived the morning of the first concert, and there was Max, waiting for us, perched on a car in the parking lot where everyone entering town had to leave their vehicle. From that moment on he was our host and tour guide, helping us carry our gear across town to our campsite in the park, entertaining us with his jokes ("There's this family of moles that lives in a hole in the ground. One day Mama Mole sticks her head up into the air and says, 'I smell pizza!' Papa Mole sticks his head up into the air and says, 'I smell cheeseburgers!' Baby Mole sticks his head up into the air and says, 'Whew! I smell mole-asses!'"), scouring the town for any additional items we might need for the weekend's festivities—sunscreen, extra ice, film, and finally, an extra twenty bucks Max found on the ground that he let us blow on beer. It was a lovely weekend, we envisioned a great future for Max, and hoped for the best for Laura.

What Max's future turned out to be was his mother's, essentially. Max never managed to emerge from the sixties, which is tough for a kid coming of age in the eighties: irreverent at school in the age of back to the basics; the first kid on the block to turn on during the war on drugs; hair to his waist in the midst of brush cuts; and a girlfriend in his bed in the garage (when Laura kicked him out of the house) instead of "family values." While the rest of us in Rositas could get by on the trappings of our former lives—as long as we had jobs and weren't on welfare—it was harder for a kid like Max, who had no history to precede him, other than ours. The times were not sympathetic. Laura told me the other day that Max was out in California getting ready to follow the Grateful Dead on their latest American tour—the only vestige left of an alternative life we thought would someday be the world's.

I danced with Laura when I regained my equilibrium.

"Who'd you get to watch Max?" I asked.

"He's over at Danny's house," Laura said. "He's been asking me if he could see Max."

"I thought you were never going to talk to Danny again after what he did to you."

"Max really misses him and I know Danny would never do anything to hurt him. Max needs a father figure, even if it's a slightly perverted one."

When Laura had broken up with the Danny under discussion, he had retaliated by breaking into her house one day and cutting one leg off all her jeans and one arm off all her blouses. It was a very graphic way of demonstrating the rupture of his broken heart.

By one o'clock Ben and I had had enough. We surveyed the remaining crowd and said our goodbyes. Carp remained on guard at the railing, drinking one more beer. Laura danced another dance, the Covingtons savored a few more minutes without Gus, and Leland and Ellen anticipated a night of wild lovemaking wherever they wanted in a childless house. As we drove down the road to Alamita to pick up our sleepy children and take them home, we speculated about their future.

"It was fun being childless for an evening," Ben said. "Maybe we should do it more often."

"Can't afford to," I pointed out. "Besides, it's a full time job inculcating them with our highly developed morality and advanced political positions. If we don't catch them now, when they're young and impressionable, their peers will twist them into greedy, materialistic monsters."

"It really pisses me off when your parents insist that Jesse is going to be a banker and Hannah a stockbroker," Ben said.

"They're just teasing."

"But they're not teasing, really. Maybe they don't think they'll be that despicable, but they're telling us, in no uncertain terms, that they're going to rebel against our values and we ultimately have no influence over them at all. Is that what they really thought about raising you?"

"Of course not. They're just trying to assuage their own disappointments by assuring us ours."

"But we're not fighting a losing battle, are we? We can't guarantee what Hannah and Jesse will do for a living, who they'll marry, what they'll wear, but we can make sure they know what's going on, can't we?"

"That's the assumption," I said.

I won't bother to tell you the particulars of what became of our kids. Suffice it to say, we can live with the results. I guess Laura and the Covingtons and the Ashleys and Carp all learned to live with their results as well. I don't think any of us want our kids to be our physical legacy to the world, but we wouldn't mind if they represented a little of our heart and soul.

The Artist as Woman

I love the grocery store in Taos. For a town of only 8,000 people, the array of them that comes through the store makes you feel like maybe you're in New York City or even Amsterdam. Of course, this eclectic mix of folks is indicative of the tourist economy that's ruining Taos, just like it's already ruined Santa Fe, but I still get a kick out of a population that runs the gamut from long-haired beautiful boys to pink-suited ski bunnies. Everyone has to eat.

Not that I know many of them. I only come into Taos to go to the grocery store or the library, maybe once or twice a week. I live out in this little village called Vallecitos where my neighbors are definitely not eclectic. They're descended from 300 year-old New Mexico families who populate all the little towns around Taos, living simple lives in quiet valleys. I see them in the store, too, but lately they're outnumbered by the ski bunnies and blond hippies.

Actually, the hippies have been around for a while. Taos got some of the first of them, way back in the early sixties, and reacted with gunfire and beatings. I must say some of newcomers probably deserved it, insensitive brutes that they were (this was before the days the women's movement added to the alternative consciousness). But after almost thirty years, things have calmed down quite a bit, at least between the hippies and indigenous people. Now we all hate the ski bunnies.

They come out to ski Taos Ski Valley, what they call a world-class resort. And now that it's a world-class resort they all want to fly into Taos, so there's a big battle brewing over expanding the airport to accommodate Lear Jets. I'm used to big battles, though, after living in New Mexico for twenty years. Out here the Wild West mentality still reigns supreme.

On this particular day in the grocery store I run into Abigail Putnam, who sometimes calls me to catch a ride into town from her rented adobe in El Rancho.

"Need a ride home, Abigail?" I ask. "I've got a little shopping to do, then I'm headed back home."

"Oh, dear, you're so kind," she answers gaily, "but I still have to go over my column at the newspaper, and then there's lunch. Care to join me?"

"Sure, where do you want to go?"

"I'm meeting Henry at The Bakery at noon. You know Henry Valencia, don't you?"

"Yeah, I know Henry, but I can't imagine why you're going to lunch with him, Abigail. He's a sexist pig."

"Oh that," Abigail waves her hand. "That's all bravado and bullshit. He just likes to shock people who think indigenous people are cultural treasure chests. Henry is big and real and in your face. I get along famously with him."

I know Henry, a foul-mouthed Chicano who works at the Taos Ski Valley setting off avalanche blasts, from our days in the Forest Service many years before. I worked as a patrol and fire lookout when Henry was the Forest Service fire management officer. He would periodically come out on my patrol route or up to the tower to try to seduce me, as he tried to seduce any woman he came in contact with. He never succeeded, at least to my knowledge, but it's rumored he actually has a live-in girlfriend who is nice and attractive, so maybe Abigail is right.

I walk to The Bakery with Abigail as she waves at almost everyone on the street. Abigail is kind of a celebrity around Taos, but for the wrong reasons. Taos knows her as an eccentric—the world knows her as a first class painter. She never shows in Taos. When I first asked her if she had a gallery in town, she answered derisively, "The galleries in Taos only want painters who specialize in the mundane. I specialize in the sublime." So she periodically takes trips back east to New York and Chicago where she displays her paintings in prestigiously sublime galleries.

The Bakery is filled with many of the longhaired beautiful boys I come to Taos to see, so even if I have to suffer Henry Valencia, it's worth it. He's already there, seated at a table, wolfing down a homegrown sandwich of sprouts, avocado, humus, tomato, and whatever else they have handy in the kitchen. As soon as we sit down, he looks at me and says, with a mouthful of sandwich, "What the hell are you doing here?"

"Thanks for that warm greeting, Henry. I'm happy to see you, too. And thanks for waiting for us."

"Abigail didn't say anything about you coming. Want to come to my house after lunch for a little R and R?"

"Henry, that sandwich looks great," Abigail says enthusiastically. "I want one of those."

"Let me do the honors, Abigail," Henry says, and yells over toward the counter, "Another number two."

I get up and order a salad while submitting a silent prayer for patience.

"I ran into Jessie at the grocery store and invited her to come along, Henry," Abigail says. "I remembered that you two used to work for that dastardly Forest Service and were great friends. I certainly am glad to see that you both quit that ragged outfit. Labor for Amerika, even if it's only lackey labor, is complicity, you know."

"Yeah, so now I just work for private capitalists making millions off the government and the people," Henry says. "Makes a lot of sense."

"But you're saving peoples' lives, Henry, which is the most important thing. Think of getting caught in an avalanche, the snow bearing down on your chest so that your very life breath is buried along with your body in that cold, cold world of death," Abigail says, eating her sandwich with gusto. "You do good work, Henry, saving all those ignorant souls."

Henry winks at me. "Abigail's politics follow a very strange rationale. But I'm glad I'm the beneficiary. Hate to be on the wrong side of this wonderful lady's wrath."

"As a matter of fact I think I'm doing my next article on the Forest Service," Abigail said. "Going to blow the lid off some timber sales around here."

Abigail writes a weekly column for one of the local papers, which contributes to her notoriety. She uses it as a soapbox, to spout off about all the things in modern society she finds distasteful, which is almost everything—except modern art, which she defends in theory, if not in practice. She gives Jackson Pollock and David Hockney a lot of slack.

"When you going back to New York, Abigail?" Henry asks. "Why don't you invite me along as your bodyguard—I'll fend off purse snatchers and homeless weirdoes trying to take advantage of a provincial from New Mexico. I haven't been to New York in about a million years."

"I can just see you in New York," I say, "ogling everything in a skirt, getting your butt beat off for the wrong ogle."

"You just want to go to New York, too, but you're too snobbish to admit it," Henry says. "I don't know what you two are doing here, anyway, especially you, Abigail. Jessie has some notion that this is hippie heaven, but you, scorned and unappreciated, could be ensconced on Park Avenue, the Pace Gallery feting you, *Art News* enshrining you."

"Let's not overdo it, Henry," Abigail says. "Even if I do sell a painting there occasionally, I'm not quite what the New York social scene has in mind for its latest emblem. Fat women in tennis shoes do better out here. Besides, I love the blue skies, clean air, and cheap rent."

"I think you're beautiful, you old bitch," Henry says, goosing her under the table. "Want to come with me and meet my mother, another old beautiful... ah, woman, like you?"

"You mean men like you actually have mothers?" I ask. "I always thought you were created by the spontaneous combustion of poisonous vapors."

"Why don't you come on out, too, Jessie, and meet the woman responsible for the monster," Henry says. "Besides, I know how all you hippie chicks like Chicano men."

"You know, Henry, I don't take being called a hippie derogatorily, as I'm sure you intend it. I'm proud to be a symbol of economic, social, and sexual freedoms."

"Henry's jealous, Jessie," Abigail says. "He's just an old repressed fart with a pony tail. Come on, let's go."

We walk out to Henry's four-wheel drive truck, emblazoned with the ski valley insignia, and drive out towards Taos Pueblo. The skies are indeed blue, and the air is filled with sunshine, not shit, but the traffic is outrageous. To get to the arterial road that runs northeast to the Pueblo, we must bypass Taos Plaza, which unlike the grocery store, only the ski bunnies venture to these days.

"I hate these fucking tourists," Henry says.

"I thought they were your bread and butter," I say.

"Yeah, when they're out on the ski slopes," he says. "Here, they're cultural genocide."

Before getting to the Pueblo, made famous by a million photographs documenting its architectural splendor, we turn off onto a dirt road that passes by old adobes with yards bare of vegetation, their hard-packed soils the perfect setting for the ubiquitous junked cars and ragged basketball hoops.

Henry stops the truck in front of an obviously new trailer.

"We've elevated Mom to the middle-class," Henry says. "And here we have another example of their good taste."

Inside, the trailer is clean and bare. A tiny old woman in a kerchief sits at a wooden table, the only kitchen furnishing besides a stove and refrigerator, her hands in her lap. Henry speaks to her in Spanish and bends down to kiss her cheek. Her mouth becomes another wrinkle that catapults her face into the realm of the mystical.

Abigail pulls up a chair, sits across from her, and suddenly the two women meld into one, gesturing and grinning and speaking nonstop. Henry, ignoring them, wanders around outside, shooting baskets and rummaging through the storage shed. I sit quietly and listen to the rhythm of their speech rather than its meaning. It's all too fast and intricate for me, but I appreciate its fervor.

When Henry appears again, his mother gets up with a smile and begins pulling out pots and pans, throwing food from the refrigerator into them, cooking like crazy. Even though we all just ate, we sit there expectantly. It's what you do.

"What were you two talking about?" I ask Abigail.

"Ah, what weren't we talking about," Abigail says. "Life, death, art, pathos, suffering, ecstasy, mothers, children."

"She asked you why I'm not married, right?" Henry says.

"Not exactly," Abigail laughs. "She asked me why you aren't married to me, a much more pertinent question. Your mother doesn't waste her energy on the trivial."

"My mother doesn't waste her energy on anything," Henry says. "She hasn't been out of this place since we moved her in. Fortunately, we all show up with supplies occasionally so she remains a person rather than a ghost."

"Why should she venture forth when all she needs to know is already in her head," Abigail says. "Now you see why I try to stay put in El Rancho. No need to muddy the clear waters."

"Coming from a yenta such as yourself, that's quite a statement," Henry says. "Spouting off in the newspaper every week isn't exactly keeping a low profile."

"That's my political duty," Abigail says. "Your mother and I know our duties to ourselves."

"Well, I know what my duty is right now, and that's to eat all this food and then get the hell out of Dodge," Henry says. "And by the way, we'd make a terrible couple, Abigail. Two old farts make one bad smell."

"Your mother was speaking theoretically, Henry, not literally," Abigail scoffs. "She, along with every other woman in the world, knows that anyone marrying you would be consigning herself to a life of unmitigated gall. She merely recognized my ability to match you blow for blow if I chose to fight. Which I don't. I'm not that masochistic."

"Vengan a comer," Henry's mother urges us, as she brings the food to the table. Bowls of stew, platters of corn, plates of bread and pastries fill the table and we gorge ourselves on the fare. Several young children run in from somewhere and join our feast. They stare shyly at Abigail and me and answer Henry's questions with giggles.

"Children should be sequestered until they're civilized enough to be around adults," Henry says. "These two belong on the funny farm. Been around my mother too long."

"You really are an old fart, Henry," I say, and then blush. "I'm sorry, Mrs. Valencia," I apologize. I have no idea if she understands English, but I'm sure she understands my intent.

"And proud of it," he says, pushing back from the table and yelling "Boo!" at the children. They run giggling out the door. "Time to hit the trail," he says. "Got to get back to work so the pigs can keep making more money."

We all take turns clasping hands with Mrs. Valencia, who smiles and bows and returns to her kitchen seat. Outside the cold air quickly dispels the lingering kitchen smells of meat and chile. As we drive back past the Pueblo Henry rolls down his window and yells, "Keep the faith, you bastards. Nobody else is gonna."

Back in town Henry drops Abigail and me off at the newspaper office. I wait while she huddles with the editor over her latest column, and then I drive her to El Rancho. Abigail's house, an unplastered three-room adobe in the middle of an alfalfa field, is cluttered with the detritus of a life in the desert— coyote and deer skulls decorate the walls; potsherds, dead cholla branches, feathers, rock crystals, dried wildflowers, and an occasional Buddha cover shelves, tables, and window sills. Surprisingly, one room is neatly arranged with stacked canvases, paints organized by color on shelves, and Abigail's paintings hanging in beautiful frames under soft lights. I've seen her work before, but her newest piece, on an easel in the middle of the room, astounds me. In warm desert colors she has depicted the plaza area of an Indian pueblo, with a kiva at each end. In the middle of the plaza sit several space ships; climbing into the kivas are composite figures of traditional and futuristic Indians. Strange bird-like animals fly through the air over their heads. It is a powerful painting, full of mystery and suspense, as life in this part of the world often is.

"Abigail, it's wonderful," I say.

"Not bad, huh?" Abigail smiles. "I really got a kick out of doing this one. Still needs some editing here and there, though. I'm not completely happy with the birds. I can't quite see yet what our birds will become."

"Are you going to send it to your gallery in New York?" I ask.

"Not this one," Abigail says. "I'm not going to let those sonsofbitches in New York use this painting to further exploit the Indian thing they think is so chic these days. This would fit right into their little scheme, and I'm not playing that game. Can't show it here, either, so I guess this one sits in my room until people's taste in art gets a little more sophisticated—hah, hah. Guess it'll be here 'till I die."

"Wish I could buy it," I say.

"You can't afford it, honey, but you can come by and visit anytime," Abigail says.

She makes us some tea and we sit out on old car seats on her porch that serve as lawn chairs. She's got a great view of Taos Mountain across the fields; clouds are rolling across the peaks, bringing a new storm to cover Henry's ski slopes with the powdery snow the pink-suited ski bunnies love so much. The sun still shines over the valley, though, where we sit, warmed by its rays.

"I wouldn't give up this view for anything," Abigail says, stretching her legs onto an adjacent chair to rest her varicose veins.

"Not even for a view over Central Park from your penthouse on Fifth Avenue?" I tease. "You really meant it when you told Henry you'd never live in New York, even if you could be a huge success?"

"I'll never be a huge success, honey," Abigail sighs. "It's not in the cards. Or should I say, it's not in my blood. I can't sell myself to the highest bidder to get there, like the cold-blooded ones do. Do you have any idea how many talented people there are out there in the world—painters, musicians, composers, writers, philosophers—living in places just as obscure as this crumbling adobe in El Rancho, who will never, ever see even the modest success that I've had in this fucked-up society that defines your worth by how much you sell yourself for? Then once you're sold they have to keep investing in you because so much money is at stake. Doesn't matter if you're old, stale, hackneyed and worthless—if some investment banker on the upper West Side bought you for thousands of dollars to hang on his wall, by God you better double or triple by the time he's ready to sell you to an investment banker on the upper East Side to hang on his wall. 'All the world's a stage and we're only the players.'"

"I wouldn't live anyplace but here either, Abigail, but it's patently unfair that you haven't made some of the money so you could live a little more comfortably—your own house, a car, security."

"I don't need that crap," Abigail says, groaning a little as she lowers her legs to the ground. "If I had a car I might never have met you or any of the other wonderful people who ferry me around. No, my only regret is that I never had children. I wouldn't mind some company in my old age."

"Were you ever married?" I ask.

"Never had that, either," Abigail says. "Not that I missed so much, judging from the divorce statistics these days. Too many Henry Valencias out there—great friends, terrible mates. Fortunately, the Henry Valencias of this world never had much interest in me, either."

We sit there in the sunlight until it's time for me to go home. I fetch Abigail a heavier coat so she can stay outside until dusk to watch the nighthawks for some inspiration for her painting. I get caught in some of the snow-bunny traffic coming down from the ski valley, but I eventually reach Vallecitos, where my husband and children wait for me, safe and sound. I don't have a wonderful painting in my living room, like Abigail does, but like they say, I guess you can't have it all.

Cleaning the Ditch

"I quit!" Lorenzo yelled and stormed out of the meeting. Everyone turned around and looked expectantly at Ben.

"I'd really rather not be mayordomo again this year," he said. "We've got a big trip planned in June, and I just don't have the time. Maybe Lorenzo will reconsider when he's calmed down."

"That loco, he gets all worked up over nothing," George said, shaking his head. "We have to have a mayordomo, it's the rules."

They'd just spent the last two hours going over a map of the village that Andre Lucero had painstakingly drawn on his computer, showing the amount of land each parciante owned and the part of the acequia each was responsible for cleaning. The reason Andre had drawn the map was because the acequia was in such bad shape that everyone had been bitching for the last two years that it wasn't fair that people who had only half or even one water right should have to clean the whole ditch, along with everyone else who owned six or seven rights. If each parciante had to clean only the part of the ditch that crossed his land, it would supposedly be more fair—large landowners should have to be responsible for more of the acequia. The ditch committee even volunteered to choose a section of ditch every year that was in particularly bad shape and help the owner get it into better shape. It all sounded right and reasonable.

Except, of course, that the way the ditches had been cleaned for the previous three hundred years had nothing to do with individual rights and fairness, it had to do with community spirit. Every parciante on the ditch helped clean the entire ditch, no matter who owned how many water rights on how much land. You just got together on the designated day in April or May, or you sent your son or your cousin, and you helped clean the ditch. Que simplicitas.

"Maybe we should forget the whole thing and just go out and clean the ditch," Ben suggested. He thought maybe he should be the voice of community spirit here.

"I spent a lot of time on this map so everyone else would quit bitching about how much work they had to do," Andre said, folding up the map and stuffing it in his pocket. "Lorenzo owns more land than anybody, so whether he likes it or not he's responsible for more of the ditch. I have five derechos myself and you don't hear me bitching."

"Maybe because he's the mayordomo, he feels like he can't handle all of it," Ben said.

"He gets paid for being mayordomo, what's he got to complain about?" George asked.

"Two-hundred and fifty bucks ain't that much for having to put up with everybody on this acequia squabbling about who's getting the water when," Vincent Griego laughed. He lived in Santa Fe and only came out to the water board meetings to represent his family's holdings. George rented the Griego land to run his cows and had to hire somebody to clean that section of the ditch.

"Then why'd he volunteer to be mayordomo this year?" George asked.

"He didn't volunteer," Ben said. "Nobody else would agree to do it."

Ben had been mayordomo for the past two years. When he told his parents, who lived back East, that he was going to serve as mayordomo, they were impressed, assuming that Ben, a white boy, must have finally been accepted by the community to be given that responsibility. When he explained to them that he was elected mayordomo by default—he was the only one on the ditch who worked at home and had the time to go out and open the presa when someone wanted more water—they insisted it still evidenced the community's trust. He didn't tell them no one could figure out what he did at home to make any money, but they didn't really care as long as he had time to be mayordomo.

For years before Ben, the same old man, Nestor Pacheco, retired from the mines in Leadville, Colorado, had been mayordomo. Not used to having time on his hands, he loved the work and relished the responsibility. Plus he knew the ditches better than anyone else in the village, being a native son who had been cleaning them since he was fourteen. He'd retired at a fairly young age and had served as mayordomo for close to twenty years. By the time Ben moved to the village, Nestor was beginning to show his age, and after he found out that Ben was home all the time, he'd stop by and pick him up on his way up to the presa, which he had to check every so often. It was way up at the end of the village, on the side of the llano, and he felt more comfortable going up there with someone else along.

Over the several years Ben went along with Nestor he became familiar with the layout of the village acequias. There were four that all came from the same river, the Rio Medio, winding its way down the valley from the high mountain peaks. It was amazing to follow the miles and miles of these ditches, laid out hundreds of years ago by the Hispano land grantees with only hand tools and intuitive engineering. Another village below had twice as many miles of ditch, fed by the same river, from the same point of diversion, to their fields four miles away. Ben was struck with the same sort of awe that he felt when he saw his first picture of the Great Wall of China. How did they ever find the individual will to do this? How did they ever have the community spirit to finish this?

Three years ago Nestor had been to the presa by himself (Ben had been in town that day, buying computer supplies, the reason he got to stay home) and had fallen and broken his leg. No one found him until that afternoon, when his wife Maria sent someone looking, and although he eventually recovered from the broken leg, Maria wouldn't let him be mayordomo anymore.

The same kind of thing was happening in other villages. In the village Ben lived in before he moved here, the same old man, Martín, had been the mayordomo for close to thirty years. When he was forced to give it up because of bad health, one of the younger men in the village took over and all hell broke loose. Everyone immediately started fighting over who was supposed to take the water when, who was taking too much, who was responsible for closing the presa, etc., etc. Instead of telling everyone to shut up and let the mayordomo decide all these questions, like Martín had always done, the new mayordomo tried to reason with everybody and be democratic. When everybody started calling Martín on the phone to ask him for the water instead of the new mayordomo, he (the new mayordomo) quit in disgust, and for the rest of the summer Martín directed the ditches from his bed.

Everyone showed up at the church the next week to get organized for the cleaning, not knowing who was going to be mayordomo. But Lorenzo was there, with Andre's computer printout in hand, figuring out who was there, who was cleaning how many sections, and which of the kids who always showed up for hire would be digging whose derecho. He seemed his old self, telling jokes and goofing on the young kids, and when they were finally assembled at the head of the ditch, Ben asked George, digging next to him, what had happened.

"Oh, he got off his high horse when he realized that if he didn't agree to the plan the committee was going to charge him a lot of money and hire someone else to do it."

"I still think we'd be better off just doing it the old way," Ben said.

"I'm not cleaning that sonofabitch's ditch," George said. "He cut Vincent's fence last year and let his cows all over the land I was leasing for my cows."

They'd been squabbling for years, over a boundary fence dispute that had escalated into total warfare. Things had gotten so bad that Lorenzo and his family no longer attended the local Catholic Church but went down the road to services in a neighboring village. Ben once asked George to explain the whole story.

"That guy makes trouble, you know," he said. "He don't get along with no one. He was okay when he was a kid growing up here, although his dad was a mean old man and we felt kind of sorry for Lorenzo having to put up with that old borracho. But when he came back from the army he was all fucked up and drinking like his old man. After awhile he got married, though, and settled down, and he went back to school on the GI Bill and learned how to be an engineer, and he got a good job down in Santa Fe. But since he got educated he thinks he's better than all of us here or something and he thinks we're all against him when really it's him who's loco. He's so crazy he thinks he can cut somebody's fence anytime he wants because he says it's in the wrong place. How does he know it's in the wrong place? Because he thinks the hay looks better over there and he wants it for his cows? He's got so much pastura up on the llano that he doesn't even have time to cut it and he goes and cuts a fence so my cows get out and I have to go chase them all over the village and he thinks we're out to get him?"

"I think he has what in English we call 'a chip on his shoulder,'" Ben said.

"He's got a cow pie for a brain," George said, shaking his head. "But nobody loses but him. We stick together. He's all alone."

It took two days to clean the acequia. Ben was done after the first day, with his measly little piece of land, and the rest of them—Lorenzo, George, Andre, and all the teenagers the other large landowners had hired to clean their sections, worked all the next day. Ben went out that afternoon, ostensibly to bring everyone a beer, but really to see how Lorenzo and George were handling the situation. Fortunately, Vincent had come up from Santa Fe so that a commissioner was present to oversee the ditch. Otherwise, you never know what might have happened.

But Lorenzo and George managed to keep out of each other's way, it seemed. All the kids were spread out between the two of them in the line, laughing, throwing weeds at each other, telling dirty jokes. George's son was working next to him, and next to him was Lorenzo's son. Ben offered them all a beer.

"You been up at your house drinking beer all day while I busted my butt out here?" George asked him, chugging his down.

"Come on, now George, you know I work hard at home," Ben said.

"Yeah, but none of us know what it is you do at home that's so hard," he said. "Hey hombres, do you know what it is this gringo does at home that he calls work?"

The two teenagers just grinned at Ben and drank their beers. They were always friendly, and waved whenever they passed each other on the road. But he suspected they, more than their fathers, considered him an outsider, even though part of them asked, why would some gringo choose to live here anyway, as they contemplated their own escape. Hopefully, that escape would only be temporary; otherwise, he worried what would become of this village without its native sons.

"You coming over to the house tonight for some chicos and chile?" George asked. "I guess we can invite you to the party even though you didn't do no work."

"Of course I'll come," Ben said. "But I thought the whole point of you guys who own all the land out here working and me who doesn't own much of anything at home resting was to make things fair."

"Forget fair," George laughed. Then he motioned for him to come over next to him, so the others couldn't hear. "As long as Lorenzo over there had to work both days and pay someone to work for his other derechos, I don't care if you sat around all day drinking tequila, mi amigo."

Lorenzo didn't come to the party, of course, but the rest of them had a great time, drinking beer and eating wonderful food that George, Andre, and Vincent's families had spent all day preparing. Andre seemed quite pleased with himself that the new system has worked so well, and everyone voted on a day when the commissioners would hire some of the teenagers to work on the section of ditch that was in the worst repair. It all seemed a little strange to Ben that they still thought this was the best way to do it after all the fighting and bickering that had gone on in preparation for the cleaning. But then fighting and bickering went on all the time anyway, so who was he to pass judgment. Ben was just glad that the acequias were still here, that people used the water to grow their hay and trees and a few vegetables, that they were all still up here, squabbling and fighting over land that was still theirs, for better or worse. And it could be a lot worse.

The Memory Care Unit

I was sitting in the dining room with Vic, my father-in-law, who was having a pretty good day, considering, when I suddenly turned around to see this startled-looking little woman sitting next to me in the wheelchair she had scooted across the room from where she started out for lunch. Her intensely blue eyes were a little teary, and she leaned forward in her chair to say to me, "I have to get away from them. Can I sit here?"

I knew where she'd been sitting previously, with one of the women who essentially doesn't speak or respond to anyone, and one of the caregivers.

"Are they ignoring you?" I asked.

"No, no I have to get away."

"Of course you can sit here," I said. I helped maneuver her wheelchair near the empty chair at our table and then she held on to the arms of her chair and started counting, "One, two, three, four, five, six, seven, eight, nine...."

I helped pull her out of her wheelchair and put her in the dining room chair. Then I went over to her former table and got her food. The caregiver didn't say a word or seem the least bit surprised that the woman had abandoned her table. I put her food in front of her.

"I can't eat this food. They want me to eat this food."

"Would you like something else?" I asked. It wasn't particularly bad food, but maybe something else might be more appealing. "Would you like a melted cheese sandwich?"

"That would be good," she said.

I asked the server to bring her a sandwich, which she did, and I introduced myself to the woman. "What's your name? My name is Rita."

She took both my hands in hers and said, "My name is Lenore. You saved my life."

Several days later when I came back to visit Vic I saw Lenore sitting in the main room with some other folks staring out the window. I went up and took her hand.

"Hello, Lenore. I'm Rita, remember me?"

She looked closely at my face and wrapped her fingers around mine. "Do I know you?"

"We met a few days ago at lunch."

"Oh, do you live here?" she asked.

"No," I laughed, "I'm just a visitor. I come to visit my father-in-law, Vic."

"Which one is he?

"He's the one over there by the desk. The one with the baseball cap."

"Oh, he must be new. I've never seen him before."

Vic had been living at the center for almost a year now, but who was I to correct Lenore. I came almost every day to visit and if I had to start anew each day, explaining myself, well, that was okay: wouldn't we all like the opportunity to reinvent ourselves occasionally?

Vic had been diagnosed with Alzheimer's almost 10 years before and had lasted at home until a year ago, when it became obvious he couldn't ever be left alone and there weren't enough of us who were able to make sure that didn't happen. While he didn't know our names anymore, he knew we belonged to him and greeted our visits with a big smile and a wave.

Whenever I came in and Vic wasn't in his room or sitting in the common room I went looking for him. And I usually found him with the maintenance man or the housekeeper, assiduously watching their work. While he couldn't really talk with them, like he used to talk with the cab driver, the barber, the security guard, the doorman, the gardener, or the plumber, he could still keep them company. Vic was a man of the people, and while Alzheimer's might be taking his tongue, it wasn't taking his affinities.

Vic, Lenore, and I joined the residents in the 11:00 o'clock sing-a-long, dredging up the words to the old standards that the group knew and loved. Vic didn't sing much, either, but I knew he knew the songs and I figured they gave him pleasure. One of the other frequent visitors led the singing, a woman who was hired by a family to spend extra time with their father, a man in his nineties who had been a well-known doctor in town. Charlene and I had become quite friendly, as we negotiated The Memory Care Unit terrain.

It turned out that she'd been the doctor's caretaker for a lot longer than his stay in The Memory Care Unit.

"Oh yes, we had some good times, John and I," Charlene said. "He owned a fishing lodge in the mountains and I helped him take care of the folks who came out and wanted a guide to take them up into wilderness. After his wife died I moved into the upstairs of his house in town and cooked and did things for him. Then last year he fell down and banged his head and couldn't remember anything and his kids decided that they were going to move him in here even though I was quite capable of taking care of him at home. But they're his kids and I'm only the caregiver, so what can you do?"

One day, after lunch, Charlene and I were talking in the hallway when Lenore showed up in her wheelchair.

"Lenore, how are you doing, dear?" Charlene asked. She had a way with the residents that expressed both camaraderie and caregiving at the same time. I felt certain that the combination was somehow able to create a category of relationship that transcended reinvention, but maybe it was all bluff. Anyway, Lenore joined us with great enthusiasm.

"Did you know that Lenore owned a boutique in New York City and sold hats for many years?" Charlene asked me.

"I had no idea," I said. "Did you grow up in the city, too?" I asked Lenore.

"I have no idea," she answered. "But that must be why I like hats so much." At the moment, she was wearing a straw one with woven Guatemalan figures sewed to the brim.

"Everyone here has a story, don't they?"

"That's right," said Charlene. "You know Phyllis, the woman with the little poodle? She was a famous mid-western artist. That's her painting on the wall over there. Some of these folks led pretty interesting lives, like my John. Did you know he was a candidate for Surgeon General at one time?"

"No. How did you end up working for him?"

"Well, I have to tell you, he kind of saved my skin. My dad, who was a doctor down in Albuquerque where I grew up, was a good friend of John's for many years. Our families used to visit and do things together. Then I moved out to Michigan to teach school and raise a family, but after about twenty years I found out my husband had a couple of other women on the side so I moved back here to New Mexico and John hired me to help him at the fishing lodge."

By this time we were sitting on the floor so we didn't have to stand there looking down at Lenore in her wheelchair. She'd been listening avidly to Charlene's story.

"You should've just told that guy to 'get out.' That's what I told my husband, 'You just get out and let me run my store without you trying to tell me to do this or that.' That's what women have to do, you know."

"You're right, Lenore, but I didn't want to stay in Michigan anyway, I was homesick for New Mexico. Maybe it was just good luck in the long run."

By this time Thelma, who could walk with a walker but was badly bent over, had joined us.

"Why hello there, Thelma," Charlene said. "You want to join our little mitote group?"

"What are you taking about?" Thelma asked. "Maybe I won't be able to contribute too much because I've only been here a couple of days and I don't know anyone yet."

I'd actually seen Thelma at the Unit for at least two months, but this was just another case of reinvention.

"Oh, it doesn't matter," Charlene said. "We're just talking about men in general, and any woman is an expert on that subject."

Just then Peter, one of the caregivers, walked by. I liked him the best of all of them because he seemed truly compassionate and not that concerned that he had to change peoples' plastic pants when they didn't make it to the bathroom on time.

"What's going on here, girls?" Peter asked, even though most of us were two or three times his age. He leaned down and kissed Lenore on the cheek.

"That's right, try and kiss all the girls and make things better," Lenore said, shaking her finger at him. "But we know what you're up to."

"I'm not up to anything, I'm just giving one of my favorite people a little kiss," Peter said.

"That's a line if I ever heard one," Thelma snorted. "Who are you, anyway?"

"Oh, Peter's not a bad sort," Charlene laughed. "Are you Peter?"

"Uh oh," Peter said. "Don't tell me this is one of those consciousness raising groups where women go around bashing men all the time."

"No, no, no," Charlene laughed. "We love men—when they do what we want them to do."

"At your service, ladies," Peter said, and began to back away.

"And don't call me a lady," Lenore said. "My name is Dotty."

One day I came around eleven to make sure I'd be there for the singing, but Charlene wasn't there and several of the Unit caregivers were attempting to lead the group anyway.

"Where's Charlene?" I asked the wife of one of the other residents, who often came for the singing, too.

She pulled me aside.

"Apparently John's family decided they didn't want to pay any extra money to have Charlene come every day and visit with John, so she's down looking for a job in Albuquerque."

"That's horrible," I said. "She's been John's caregiver for over 20 years."

"That's right. John won't come out of his room if she's not here."

"Why is she down in Albuquerque looking for a job? Isn't the family providing her with a pension or something?"

"I don't know. I only heard about this from listening to several of the caregivers talking to each other about it."

I didn't have any way to get in touch with Charlene, but every day I made sure I went into John's room to say hello and sit for a few minutes. He was almost completely blind and deaf, but he appreciated the company. Then one day Charlene came in while I was sitting with Vic, and she beckoned me into John's room.

"What happened, Charlene? How could the family cut you off at this stunningly complex moment?"

"They're all stunningly complex moments, honey," she said. "I think they just figure that if I'm not here John will fade away a little quicker."

"That's horrible."

"Well, it's horrible and it's not so horrible. They don't much like seeing their once vibrant and prosperous dad so debilitated."

"Maybe it's the 'once prosperous' part they're so worried about," I said.

"I'm sure that's part of it, but they're all grown up and have money of their own, so I'm going to be charitable and think it's the part about not wanting to see him continue to decline and lose all quality of life."

"I know, I have to watch the same thing happen to Vic."

"That's where we're all headed, I'm afraid."

"Unless we decide to do something about it beforehand."

"We can make all the beforehand decisions we want," Charlene sighed. "But until the time is actually at hand, we'll never know."

"Did you find a job?"

"Not yet, but I'll figure something out. Would you do me a favor, though, and check on John when you come to visit Vic, and make sure he goes in to eat lunch?"

"Of course I will. Do you have to go to Albuquerque to look for work? Can't you find something here so you can come visit occasionally?"

"It's too expensive to live here. Besides, John's family told the staff not to let me visit John more than once every two weeks. They want him to forget who I am."

Before I could say anything she lifted her hand. "Let's not go there. Just promise me you'll check in on John when you can."

I did check in on John whenever I came to visit, but several months later Vic contracted pneumonia and quickly died. I thought I would continue to go over and visit Lenore and John and Phyllis and Thelma, but life got in my way and I haven't been back for a while now. My familiarity with The Memory Care Unit elicited many more conversations like the one I had with Charlene, about "doing something beforehand," but we all came to the same conclusion she did: We'll never know until the time is actually at hand. And then it may be too late.